GOING DEEPER

WOLF APPEAL BOOK 3

KB ALAN

To my all of my GBG95-96 sisters, especially my Visalia 2018 crew (and Jed). Your support, encouragement and enthusiasm means the world to me. We are so strong when we're together and I love you to the moon and stars. To my housemates (and Jed), I will be laughing about that night when I'm an old lady who can't get out of her rocker. What a gift. I love you all (and Jed)!

ABOUT THIS BOOK

Going Deeper

The opportunity to be one of the first members of a brand new werewolf pack is an exciting adventure for lifestyle blogger Cindy McCarthy. With her best friend by her side, she's ready for anything.

Jonas visits New Mexico to see this brand new pack in action and make sure it's a good home for his parents to retire to. Instead, he finds Cindy, and suddenly the visit takes on a whole new purpose. He's almost certain she's his mate, meant to be his forever.

Opening their souls to each other is only the beginning. They'll need to navigate setting up a new life together, with a new pack. One that has old dramas to put to bed and new relationships to forge. If Alicante can come together as a pack—a family—they all might survive the adventure intact.

To join KB Alan's newsletter, visit www.kbalan.com/newsletter
Subscribers will receive a link to download a free copy of Past Perfect, a prequel to the Perfect Fit series

CHAPTER ONE

Holding her breath, Cindy eased open the oven door and peeked inside. Then let the door drop with a thud when she saw what was waiting for her. It was her second attempt at making the apple bread recipe, and the second failure.

Grabbing the potholders that matched her pretty lemon-printed apron, she pulled the loaf pan out of the oven and set it on the counter. The "loaf" looked like an incredibly soggy pile of brown... well, it looked highly unappetizing.

Ah well, it was time to declare the recipe a failure. The question was, should she inform the company that had sent it to her—asking her to feature it on her blog—that she wasn't going to be able to accommodate them, or post the recipe, showing pictures of the failed results, asking her readers to do their own tests and report back with outcome? Decisions, decisions.

She was glad she'd tried the recipe now, in her familiar oven. If it had failed in her new oven, once she moved, she'd have wondered if the appliance was to blame.

Grabbing her camera, she took several shots of the mess, just in case. She wasn't against posting failures, sometimes they were appreciated by her readers, but she preferred to be able to end the post with success, or be able to identify what she thought was wrong with the recipe. Well, she'd give it some thought, but had the pictures recorded if she needed them.

Leaving the pan to cool before she attempted cleaning it out, she hung up her apron and went to her office. While the kitchen looked spotless and beautiful, in her ever-so-humble opinion, the office looked like a disaster, with moving boxes piled high and her desk empty of everything except the computer and printer. The bookshelves were all packed up, and she'd decided to work on the linen closet next. She put the camera on the empty bookshelf and grabbed the tape gun and large marker.

When the phone in her pocket rang with her mother's ringtone, she tried not to grimace. And failed. She plucked her earbuds out of her pocket and plugged them in before pressing the button to accept the call. No way was this going to be a short conversation.

"Hi, Mom."

"Cynthia, how come I had to hear from your aunt Laura that you've rented your house out?"

"I told you I decided to rent it out instead of selling it."

"Yes, but not that you'd found someone."

"It's a nice house in a good location, especially for another pack member. I told you I didn't think it would take long to find someone."

Her mother ignored that reminder. "I'm still not convinced this is a good idea."

"Flying to see you in Texas won't be much different if I'm coming from Arizona than when I come from St. Louis."

"I know, it's not that. But what can Myra be thinking, leaving her pack? They love her, and I thought she loved being alpha of St. Louis. An alpha can't just up and leave her pack on a whim, it's not natural."

"If her mate had been anyone else, certainly another alpha, one of them would have had to leave their pack, and you wouldn't have thought anything of it."

"I don't think I trust this Adam character," Dana said, switching tacks.

Cindy bit her tongue, figuratively, and counted to five. "You haven't even met him."

"It's not right that he's been in hiding all these years. What does he have to hide? A strong alpha, a good one, should have been part of a pack."

"Mom. You know he was turned against his will. Why would he then jump right into pack life with a bunch of werewolves, after being viciously attacked by them?"

"That rogue pack was not normal and you know it." The indignation in her mother's voice was clear and had Cindy rolling her eyes as she taped the bottom of a box closed and flipped it over. She took it to the linen closet and studied the contents.

"I do know it. It was crazy and I still can't believe it happened, but it did. But he had no way of knowing that, so why would you be surprised that he stayed away from anything werewolf until he found out otherwise?"

"If he's smart, it shouldn't have taken him so long."

Cindy sighed. "Mom, when you heard that Zach out in Mountain View had found his mate the same way, finding Hillary, who'd been avoiding wolves since she was attacked by those same crazy people, you didn't mistrust *her*. You were sympathetic and worried about her."

"It's not the same."

"Why? I think you're being sexist."

Her mother sputtered, but Cindy thought she was on to something. "You hold Adam to a different standard than you did Hillary. If Myra hadn't decided to leave St. Louis, Adam would be coming here to be my alpha anyway. So what's the difference if I choose to go to Arizona, and they are too, and so they're my alphas there instead of here?" She was genuinely confused about her mother's problem.

Dana sighed. "It's time you came back home to Texas. There's no reason to move to another state again."

"Ah." She put the box down and flopped onto the couch. That was so not happening. Ever. And she was shocked her mother wanted it to happen.

"It's embarrassing that you make like our pack's not good enough for you."

Cindy tried, in vain, to formulate a response to that ridiculous statement, but her mother forged on.

"You know that Brenda wouldn't be a problem if you came back home, right? Whatever issues you girls had in the past, I'm sure you could—"

"Mom," Cindy interrupted. "It's not about Brenda. I like the idea of helping to build a new pack from scratch. I don't know that I'll ever go back to Texas."

When she'd moved eighteen years ago, it hadn't been because of her old boss, Brenda, though she supposed her mom would see it that way. Her first job out of college hadn't gone well, mostly because she'd lost respect for her boss, who happened to be the fourth in her pack's hierarchy. The respect issue had been about Brenda's business decisions, but she couldn't deny that it carried over into her respect of the woman as a pack leader.

The hierarchy was the pack leadership, with the pack alpha at the top—two, if they were mated—and then the first, second, third and fourth, down from there. The ranking was based purely on power, with each wolf or mated pair taking different responsibilities in the running of the pack. If Cindy had chosen to stay, it would have been a bit of effort to not let that lack of respect show amongst the pack, but she could have done it.

"Really, I didn't leave because of Brenda. I told you, once I started looking for another job, I realized that the whole country was available to me, and I liked the idea of trying out somewhere new." She had, in fact, told her parents that several times.

"You didn't even keep the job in St. Louis for very long before quitting," Dana said, as if that meant the choice to move there had been a mistake.

"No, because the blog took off in a way I never could have foreseen. It gave me an interesting challenge for a long time, but now it runs so smoothly, I think changing things up again will be good for me. Call it my midlife crises if you want."

"Cynthia, you're only forty-one."

"The perfect age to try something new. It's not like there's a risk to it, Mom. My job is very stable and successful and I can do it from anywhere in the country. Heck, I could go to Europe if I wanted to."

"You need to stop gallivanting around and find your mate."

Cindy sighed, but not audibly. How in the world her mother could sound insulted over this conversation was beyond Cindy. And wasn't gallivanting around going to make her more likely to find her mate than staying home, where she already knew her mate *wasn't?*

Having no idea how to respond, she just waited.

"It's not too late to have children, you know."

This time, she let the sigh be audible. "I don't have a whole lot of control with the whole finding-my-mate thing, Mom. You can't blame me for that one. And traveling around, meeting more packs, that will help with my chances, don't you think?"

Werewolves knew pretty quickly when they'd met their mates. They could have relationships before that, but they usually didn't last long, as both parties knew it wasn't the real thing. She'd enjoyed several relationships, but none longer than eight months. And it was very rare for a werewolf to get pregnant from anyone other than their mate, so even her mother couldn't blame her for not producing grandchildren.

"That's true." Apparently this was a new idea to her mom, because Dana's voice brightened at the idea. "You said you were going to help Myra interview some of the wolves who wanted to join the new pack?"

"That's right." Myra, her best friend for sixteen years, was her current alpha. She'd been the one to shut down the Mesa Pack when Hillary had mated Zach, and it had been discovered that there was a rogue pack doing horrific things out in Arizona. It had been Myra's job as the National President, elected to serve a one-year term as the head werewolf in the United States, to determine the fates of every member of both packs. She'd had to condemn to death the wolves who had been actively involved in abducting, attacking and murdering people in the supposed effort to turn them into werewolves. Since that wasn't how werewolves were turned, it wasn't a surprise to any sane wolf that the process hadn't worked most of the time, and only two people had survived—Hillary and Adam—several years apart.

Cindy couldn't imagine sentencing anyone to death, but then again, her friend was the alpha for a reason. Personally, Cindy was happy to be a typical werewolf, not part of the hierarchy, let alone an alpha. The idea of choosing who would die versus who would be sent to other packs seriously made her nauseous. But Myra had handled it, finding homes for those who weren't to die, working with the pack alphas across the country to determine the best situation for every one of the wolves.

Then she'd gone on a search for Adam, knowing only that a single wolf besides Hillary had survived being attacked by the rogue pack, and wanting to find him and ensure that he was living a safe and healthy life.

Cindy would never forget the moment her best friend discovered that the man was her mate. She shivered at the thought of that level of emotion ever going through her. Although maybe it wouldn't be as extreme, since alphas were generally hit by the magic of the mate bond more strongly than the average wolf.

"You'll come visit when we get settled," she invited. Her parents had only visited St. Louis once in all the years she'd been there, so she felt fairly safe in issuing the invitation. "We're just going to rent for a while, make sure the area we choose is a good selection for the whole pack. There are a lot of things to consider, and we may not find the right town the first go."

"All right, I guess that will do. I'll let you get to your packing and tell your father you said hello."

"Thanks, Mom. And give my love to Bill, Juanita, and the kids when you see them." Her brother and his wife were frequent visitors to her parents' house, a fact that amazed her. She swore it was like she and her brother had completely different parents. For sure, they had completely different relationships with them.

She hung up and switched the phone to music, then went at the linen closet with renewed vigor. Maybe she couldn't articulate exactly why this move felt like the right thing, but she was certain that it was. She'd been very seriously considering the idea even before she'd mentioned it to Myra and discovered that her best friend was thinking the same thing. That had just solidified it for them both, and nothing since had led her to question the decision.

Meeting Adam, shortly after he and Myra had mated, made it clear how right the decision had been. She'd instantly felt comfortable with him, and looked forward to him being her alpha and to helping him understand that he was meant to be a leader of wolves, not a loner.

After the linen closet, she tackled the guest bathroom. She had some friends coming over tomorrow to help with the kitchen and move the boxes into the container she'd rented, one that would be transported to their destination when she was ready. In the meantime, they just needed to explore a couple of cities and make a decision on where to begin.

JONAS GROANED when the phone rang with his mother's ringtone. He loved his mother, but she refused to acknowledge that his current job as a bartender, almost always covering the closing shift, should influence what time she decided to chat. The fact that he was in a time zone three hours behind hers also seemed to make little impact.

He accepted the call and brought the phone to his ear, flinging his other arm over his eyes. He kept meaning to get better drapes, but…well, who really wanted to go drapery shopping? Not him.

"Hi, Mom."

"Jonas, is it really necessary to grumble at me like that when I call?"

"Only when you call at seven-thirty, and I didn't go to bed until three."

"It's ridiculous that you have a job that keeps you out until three in the morning. But it's hardly my fault."

He wasn't going to go there. While his parents weren't actively against his move to a slower-paced life three years ago, neither were they impressed with his decision to take a job they considered beneath him. They seemed to have missed that the whole point in selling his business as a high-end recruiter in New York City was to try life at a more relaxed pace.

Joining the Mountain View pack, in Idaho, had been the right choice. And the job at the pack's bar—one they worked to keep wolf only, no humans—was perfect. He had little to no stress and enjoyed interacting with his fellow pack members. It had been a great way to get to know them better. Though they were a friendly enough bunch, they didn't get a lot of new members who weren't mates, so his wandering in and becoming part of the group had been greatly helped by accepting the job as bartender.

Since he had chosen not to respond, his mother apparently decided to move on.

"Your father and I are thinking of moving."

"What?" They'd been in their house since before he'd been born. "Is there a problem or something? You know if you need help…"

Her voice softened at his offer. "No problem, it's just like you said, time to consider a new pace in life. We've been in the city forever but it's not such a great place to retire, we're thinking."

"Wait. You're not just moving houses, but out of the city? Where are you thinking?"

"Arizona."

"What?" This time it was more of a shout than a question. He dropped his arm from his face and sat up so fast, his head swam a bit. His parents had always lived in New York. *Their* parents had always lived in New York. They'd acted like he was crazy when he'd said he was leaving.

"We think the dry air would be good for your father's arthritis. Besides, it's exciting, this new pack. Myra Talmidge was out your way, did you meet her? What did you think?"

He blinked at the unexpected change of direction that he should have seen coming. "No, I didn't meet her. I did meet her mate, Adam. Played a game of pool with him but he was starting a bit of a mating frenzy, from being separated from Myra, so I don't suppose it's a good experience to judge him on. Still, I'd say he's probably a good guy. No experience being alpha, but it's in him, no question. He's strong."

"That's good to know. We emailed Myra and we'll see what happens. I'm sure she'll want some experienced elders in her pack." Her voice was a bit uncertain.

"I think you're probably right, Mom, I just want to make sure it's the right decision for you. You've never talked about leaving New York."

"We are getting older, you know. And while I still think it's a bit ridiculous that you retired at your age, at our age it's acceptable."

He let the dig go, not interested in rehashing a decision that had already been made, and had turned out to be an excellent one, in his opinion.

"We want to try it out, while we're young enough to enjoy the change. Plus, if we decide we hate living somewhere without snow, we can always come back."

"True. Listen, Myra's become good friends with Zach and Larry. Why don't you let me get in touch with her, have a chat, see what they're thinking with all this."

"Honey, I don't think you should call your alpha that name."

He just laughed. "You'll have to meet her sometime, Mom. In the meantime, let me have a chat with Myra or Adam, or both of them, and feel things out a bit."

"That would be nice, Jonas. Thank you."

"You bet. I'll let you know what I find out."

He disconnected and let the idea simmer a bit. It actually wasn't a bad one. In their early seventies, it was true his parents should start thinking about where they wanted to live out their retirement, and somewhere without the bother of snow would be good. Although there were always younger pack members ready to make a buck shoveling out the elders' driveways, his parents liked their independence, and he could see how they might appreciate not having to rely on others for tasks they'd handled their whole lives.

Rolling off the bed, he scratched and stretched and reached for the sweatpants hanging off the end of the mattress, pulling them on. There was no way he was getting back to sleep, so he might as well roll with it. Besides, he had the day off.

He quickly poached a couple of eggs and decided to head out to the pack house, see who was around for a run. If he was lucky, since it was the weekend, one of his alphas would be there and he could ask their opinion on the matter. If not, he'd track them down later and take the time to let the idea work in his brain.

The pack house was alive with the wolves who lived there as well as several other pack members like himself, who were interested in a group run. Zach, in wolf form, was playing with a group of adolescents on the grass, and Jonas had to smile at their antics. He went into the house and found a spot for his clothes, then made the shift. He ran into Stephen, their second, on his way off the porch, and they raced into the woods together. The other man beat him in the long run, but it was a good chase.

He enjoyed this adopted pack, had made several friends, but he did need to start considering a permanent situation. He liked his job, but he'd taken it on as a favor to fill a vacant slot. Was it what he wanted to do for the foreseeable future? Maybe, maybe not. He was renting a small apartment that he'd found when he'd first hit town three years ago, and had intended to stay in only shortly, while he got a feel for the place. Inertia had kept him there, but maybe he should consider finding a more permanent home.

Not entirely sure how he'd gone from contemplating his parents' future to his own, he took a short nap in the sun with several of his packmates, at home with the group, and yet suddenly not certain he was really home.

CHAPTER TWO

Cindy was going to start bawling any minute, she just knew it. She was trying not to, was worried it would send the wrong message. She and Myra were committed to starting the new pack, but she hadn't considered how hard it would be to actually watch Myra, her alpha, hand over the pack that she had lovingly led for so long.

Myra held Adam's hand tightly as she stood before Kendra and Deacon, with most of the pack spread out around the group, on the back lawn of the pack house. Cindy could see Adam's knuckles were white. It would be odd for him, she supposed, to be feeling some of the connections of the pack to his mate, but not the normal level, since he was not their alpha.

He and Myra had left Mountain Pack after their mating and gone to his cabin in Montana to spend a couple of weeks together, alone. Now they'd come back to officially hand the reigns over to St. Louis' firsts, who would be the new alphas.

Cindy knew that they were making the right decision, but it was still hard to see her friend stepping aside, though she was thrilled to see Deacon and Kendra stepping into the rolls of alpha. They had been the packs firsts for several years now, and were more than ready for their new responsibilities.

She watched as Myra released her mate and put one hand on each of her firsts' shoulders. Her view was of Kendra and Deacon's faces, not Myra's, but she imagined her friend had closed her eyes and was concentrating on the power that connected her to the pack. She saw the moment that it hit Kendra and Deacon, felt it as well. After all, she was still a member of the pack. She'd experienced it when she'd moved from Texas to St. Louis, felt the cutting of the tie between herself and her previous alpha in a way that wasn't exactly uncomfortable, but jarring.

Because she already had a bond with Kendra and Deacon, as members of the hierarchy of her pack, she was able to feel the pulse in the thread between them that would solidify when she approached them as a member.

Except, she wouldn't. It was best that she move forward with Myra and Adam at this point, finally creating the little pack that they'd been working towards for a month.

Myra stepped away, into Adam's waiting arms, and Cindy moved to stand near them. They watched as each pack member made their way to their new alphas, to receive a hug or a handshake, a touch to solidify the connection that now bound them.

Cindy glanced at Adam to see how he was taking it all in. The wolf had been a loner since being turned, had never lived with a pack, never been bound to anyone, either as leader or subordinate. He'd wrapped his arms around Myra and was watching the scene intently.

When about half of the pack had gone to their new alphas, Myra caught Cindy's gaze and motioned her back. The three of them made their way out of the yard and to the edge of the wood. Myra gave her mate a kiss, then pulled free and gave Cindy a long hug, re-cementing their bond. Cindy felt the burst of love and loyalty like a warm balm to her soul.

She turned to Adam, who winked at her. Laughing, she stood in front of him and let him decide how he wanted to proceed. Being his first pack member was an honor that she didn't take lightly, and she felt like her heart was in her throat.

He reached a hand out to her shoulder, let it rest there for a moment as he watched her.

She saw emotion hit his eyes just before he pulled her into a tight hug. The connection pulsed into place, a warm and welcoming one that satisfied a need in her to belong to her alphas. He drew back and kissed her cheek, before winking at her once again. She laughed and let Myra's joy wash through her.

"Our new pack. So small, but precious," Myra said.

"Was that totally weird?" Cindy asked Adam.

"Totally. But also pretty cool."

"Now we just need a place to live," Myra said.

"Details, details," Cindy said with a careless wave of her hand.

"Says the details queen," Myra laughed.

"We'll figure it out. I'm all packed up and ready to go. Let's make a plan."

"The fourth in Los Angeles is interested in moving, and she's a security specialist. I'd love to get someone with those skills in from the beginning, if she's a good fit," Myra said. "Her name is Jen. There's also a mated pair of seconds from Denver, an older couple from New York thinking to retire, and another handful of non-hierarchy from all around the country. There's more that have asked to be kept updated."

"I'll start a post on the forum letting people know what decisions have been made. Send me the names of those who want to be updated and I'll direct them to the post," Cindy suggested.

"Perfect. And we're all agreed to try Alicante, New Mexico, first, right?"

"It looks like a good spot, and I kind of like the idea of settling in New Mexico, instead of Arizona, if the town works out," Adam said. "That's definitely something you can update on the forum, Cindy. People are still assuming we'll go back to Arizona."

"I like it," Cindy said. "And the research I've been doing on Gila National Forest looks beautiful. I'll do a post with some pictures."

"Then that's what we'll do," Myra said. "We're packed as well. I think we should go ahead and head out tomorrow. It will be confusing to the pack to have me here much longer."

"It's a plan," Cindy said.

CINDY DECIDED she was in love. The town of Alicante was more than she'd hoped, and she really believed they would be able to settle their pack there. It boasted about ten thousand people and was large enough for a grocery store, some restaurants, a couple of antique shops, an art gallery and a bar. No Target, movie theater or mall, but those were less than an hour away. And there was hardly any traffic, which was awesome.

She was also half in love with her landlady, a spry seventy-three-year-old widow who rented out the house she used to share with her husband, while she lived with her daughter and son-in-law, helping them care for their kids.

Myra and Adam had found a place outside of town, deeper in the forest, that would work well as a pack house, and had been able to rent it. The owner had indicated a desire to sell, which might prove handy if they decided to stay in Alicante. Two weeks in and they had a solid idea of what it would take to support a small pack, and how they could expand and grow that pack in the future. It was time to start meeting potential members.

They had decided to throw a party. Well, okay, it had been her suggestion, which Myra loved and Adam balked at. But she'd asked him whether he'd prefer one party over in a few hours, or many meetings with many people, over the course of days. He'd seen the logic of her option, then.

Of course, she couldn't just throw a party and not make it part of her work. So she had to pick a theme and run with it, take lots of pictures, blog about the results. She also needed a signature drink for the party, which had amused Adam to no end, but he'd helped her out and they'd settled on a Full Moon Mash, a take on a margarita with muddled cactus pear. Adam had been skeptical, but had enjoyed the testing, as well as the results.

She'd helped them get the house pulled together quickly, so that they could host the party there. The living room, dining room, kitchen and library/office were set.

The full moon was tonight, which made it extra fitting. They would mingle, eat, and then go for a run together, exploring the woods. She was pretty sure that would be enough to have a solid idea about most of the guests.

It had been a long time since she'd been anxious about a party, but she wanted to make everyone feel welcome and comfortable. She wanted their tiny pack to present well, and while intellectually she knew that had nothing to do with whether or not people liked her subtle decorations or her signature cocktail, emotionally it was all tied together and she wanted it to be perfect.

Adam opened the door for her and ran his hand up and down her arm, soothing the nervousness she hadn't realized had increased so much. She took a deep breath and tried to shake it off. She trusted Myra and Adam. No one who didn't fit well with their group would be asked to join, she was sure of that. There was no reason to be jittery.

Actually, there was one reason. Two of the people coming to the party were from the original Mesa pack. Well, one was a teenager, but her mother, Olivia, had been part of the pack that had allowed the rogue Phoenix pack to exist. Adam had told her he was willing to meet the woman and give her a chance, but she and Myra were both ready to reject the pair if Adam felt the least bit conflicted about them joining. Still, he didn't seem worried, so she tried to put it out of her mind.

She put the final touches on the decorations and took a look around. The large dining room was what had sold them on the house. It was big enough to hold a table that could sit twelve comfortably, a few more if they got cozy. The landlord had painted it a pretty dove gray, and they'd bought chairs upholstered in a soft mauve that looked perfect in the room.

As might be expected in a house with such a dining room, the kitchen was excellent, boasting lots of cabinets and plenty of counter space. The appliances weren't top of the line, not what she would buy for herself, but they were decent enough for a rental and had handled the party needs handily. If the pack ended up buying the house, she supposed they'd upgrade over time.

The living room was open, with enough room for a couch, love seat and two chairs near the fireplace, and a smaller sitting area by the back door, which led to a spacious patio.

She helped Adam haul the meat to the barbecue outside and get it fired up, and tasted the guacamole that Myra was putting out as the first guests arrived. She took a deep breath and went out to meet her potential new packmates.

An hour later, she was laughing with Jen, the fourth from Los Angeles, who was telling her a story about getting stuck in a strange city, naked. She glanced over at Adam to see how he was doing, but he seemed completely at ease as he spoke to a couple from Florida. It amused her that her alpha had ever thought he wasn't a people person, when he was such a natural leader.

She'd opened her mouth to respond to Jen when a scent hit her. Something about it was so intriguing she forgot what she was about to say and turned her head to find the source.

A man was standing at the door with an older couple, the group obviously having just arrived. Myra was introducing herself and leading them into the house. The man looked around, met Cindy's gaze—and stopped walking. The woman with him grabbed his arm impatiently and tugged him along, out of the room.

Cindy blinked, turning back to Jen, who simply raised an eyebrow at her.

"Know them?" Jen asked.

"No, you?"

"Not a clue. He's hella handsome, though."

"Yes, yes he is."

"I need another drink," Jen said, holding up her empty margarita glass. "You want anything?"

"I'm still good, thanks." She turned to see who she should talk to next, to find a woman and teenager walking up to her.

"Excuse me, are you Cindy? I'm Olivia Keogh, and this is my daughter, Tasha. We were led to believe the new pack was going to be in Arizona, but you seem to be settling here, in New Mexico."

The words were just shy of being argumentative, which Cindy thought was a bit cheeky, but she just smiled. This was the woman she'd been concerned about meeting Adam.

"The territory for the old pack was all of Arizona and half of New Mexico. That's a lot of territory to choose from, and to see what works best for the new pack."

"So you're not intending to let the old pack members of Mesa, the ones innocent of any wrongdoing, go back to their homes?"

"Mom," Tasha mumbled in protest.

"The innocence—or lack thereof—of the pack members has already been decided by the National President at that time. That has nothing to do with settling a new pack. Any wolf in the country interested in joining the new pack is welcome to make their interest known. That's why you were invited to this party, Olivia. Your email didn't make any mention of wanting to return to a specific area."

The woman's lips pursed tightly. "We had to sell our house."

Cindy nodded. "That was probably very distressing. Where have you settled?"

"She sent us to Chicago," Olivia said, visibly trying to suppress her annoyance. "We don't like the snow."

"I'm sorry to hear that. Even if you don't choose to join our pack here, you can petition the National President to join another."

"He's said that he won't be making any changes to the Mesa Pack members until they've been in place twelve months," Tasha interjected, putting a hand on her mother's arm.

"That makes sense," Cindy mused. "Gives everyone a chance to try and settle in before making any further moves. To ensure they give their new pack a fair try, and the new pack gives them the same." She felt for the girl, who was clearly embarrassed by her mother.

"It means my daughter would be uprooted again. Nobody seems to be considering the children in this mess," Olivia argued.

Cindy didn't really see how that would be different if the Keogh's moved now, or after the year was up, but it didn't seem like the right time to argue the issue. "That's a good point. If you decide you'd like to join us, feel free to mention that to Myra and Adam, I'm sure it would be an important consideration. If you'll excuse me, it looks like we need more chips." She gestured to the table laden with food, gave an encouraging smile to Tasha, and walked to the kitchen.

Okay, maybe she could have handled that better, but she'd liked the girl and wanted to give her a chance.

She opened the pantry and pulled out a bag of tortilla chips, ripped it open and stuck one in her mouth as she headed back out. And nearly walked into the man she'd seen entering the house not long ago.

"Mmph, sorry," she mumbled around her food, managing to stop just short of his chest.

"No need." His voice was deep, and it sent a tiny shiver down her spine.

She blinked up at him and stared. His eyes were grayish-green with a dark green circle around the iris. She blinked again, blushed at having been staring at his eyes, and managed to swallow her chip without choking on it.

He smiled at her, and she was pretty sure her heart skipped a beat. His dark brown hair flopped over his forehead in messy curls that she wanted to brush through with her fingers.

"Any idea where a guy might find a bottle opener around here?" he asked, holding up a dark ale.

She frowned, having left two of the darn things on the drinks table. "Yes, they should be over here somewhere," she said, leading the way back to the table. She found one underneath a damp napkin and held it out for him, then searched out the second one, which had somehow ended up behind the tub of ice and beer.

"Thanks, you're a life saver. My name's Jonas. Jonas Toland." He held his hand out to her after wiping the dampness from the bottle onto his jeans.

"Cindy McCarthy." She took his hand—and felt a burst of warmth deep in her belly.

He squeezed gently, then rubbed at her hand a bit with his thumb. A move she'd found gross from another man years before now felt like just the thing she needed to know that this guy was as interested in her as she was in him.

The sound of someone clearing their throat next to her startled her. She pulled on her hand, but he didn't release it, merely turned his attention to Adam and Myra, who'd walked up to them. Adam introduced Myra, and only when Jonas had to shake the alpha's hand did he release his hold on Cindy.

"So, Jonas. You're thinking about moving packs?" Adam asked. "You didn't mention anything when I was in Mountain View."

"Well, no, I wasn't. My parents are thinking of leaving New York, though. I met them here, wanted to introduce them to you, give them a chance to take a look around." He motioned to the older couple he'd come in with, in deep conversation with someone on the other side of the room. "Where are you from, Cindy? Are you thinking of joining up with this lot, too?"

"Actually, I already have."

"She's our first official member. And my best friend," Myra told him.

"New Mexico's charms are growing on me," Jonas said, his gaze on Cindy filled with a heat that she felt like a brand.

"Well. Okay then," Adam said. "We'll just go introduce ourselves to your parents."

"I would love if we can get some elders to join," Myra said. "A pack needs the right balance of experience and youth, wisdom and energy."

Jonas nodded, but didn't say anything. Didn't take his eyes off Cindy.

"Maybe you'd like a tour of the house," she suggested.

"Absolutely, if you're the one giving it."

She offered her hand, girlishly pleased when he took it without hesitation and followed her out of the room.

JONAS TOOK the offered hand of the gorgeous wolf in front of him. She turned and led the way out of the crowded room, down a hallway and into a room that was clearly being set up as a library. He resisted the urge to tug on the hair that hovered a bit above her shoulders, sort through the strands that seemed to vary between rich brown and gold. She was holding his hand, and that was going to have to be good enough...for now.

He'd never wanted to bury his nose in someone's neck so soon after meeting them before. Could she be his mate? If so, he was ready, willing and able, that was for sure. Her bright blue eyes had called to him from across the room, and he'd waited until she'd detached herself from first one woman, then a pair of them, and had headed into the kitchen alone. He'd made his move, only to be caught off guard with the punch-to-the-gut sensation when he was close to her. And when he'd shaken her hand. And gotten a good whiff of her amazing scent.

Damn, if she wasn't his mate, he still wanted her.

He listened to her explain how they were setting the room up to be a good place for kids to do schoolwork and young adults to take online courses if they wanted to learn a new skill. It was fairly standard for a pack house, so he just nodded, letting her talk through her nerves. He couldn't deny he was feeling a bit of the butterflies as well.

Was this it? Was she the one?

He wanted to know, but found he was sort of enjoying the mystery.

"You guys have accomplished a lot in a short amount of time," he complimented.

"It was a lot of work, but we thought it was important for people coming to the party to feel they're being welcomed into a real pack house, not a temporary or transitory situation."

"So you feel pretty sure this will be the permanent home? Alicante, I mean."

"I think so. It's early, I know, but it does feel right. It's always possible we'll need to move for some reason, but so far, we're pleased."

"It's such an odd thing, starting a pack from scratch like this." He leaned against the back of the couch, still holding her hand, but resisting further touch. For now.

"It really is. It's kind of cool being involved from the beginning, I'm enjoying it."

"It must feel good to have your opinion so valued by your alphas."

She blushed. "I probably shouldn't admit to it, but it does. Myra's been my alpha for a long time, and my best friend for nearly as long, so I know she trusts me and values my opinion. But this does take it to a new level, and that feels really good. And I've enjoyed seeing Adam find his way to being a true alpha. It's wonderful to witness."

"Yeah, when I met him in Mountain View and heard he was a lone wolf, I was astonished. He reads so clearly alpha, I'm amazed he made it that long without trying to be in charge of people and fix all their problems."

She laughed and nodded. "Right?" She swallowed, her gaze focused on his face, captivating him so that he almost missed her free hand coming up to touch his chest. Her breathing picked up. "This seems...important, doesn't it?"

He liked that she wasn't shying away from it. "Yes. We have two choices. Take things slow and enjoy the journey as much as the destination. Or jump at it full throttle and see where we end up." In that moment, he couldn't say what he hoped she would answer. Knew only that he would win, either way. And so would she.

She swallowed, let her eyes drift down for a moment, then met his again. "Let's go slowly. For now. But I reserve the right to change my mind at any time."

He couldn't help it. He laughed, pulled her into his body and wrapped his arms around her. His chin rested naturally on top of her head, and he took in a huge breath. He would enjoy the journey.

"Can I take you to dinner tomorrow?" he asked, opening his arms so she could pull back and see his face. He wished he could take her tonight, but they'd be too tired after the run, and it would be late.

"That would be nice. Or maybe lunch would be better," she suggested.

"Somewhere public would be good. To help me keep my word."

She gave him a saucy grin. "I'll pick the place." She pulled his cellphone out of his back pocket, turned it on and quickly found the messages app while he watched. She sent herself, he assumed, a message, and returned the phone to his pocket.

"I should get back to the party. I haven't met everyone yet and we'll be changing for the run soon."

"I don't know if this counts as much of a tour," he complained.

"That just means you'll have to come back for more," she tossed over her shoulder as she headed out of the room.

He stayed where he was, breathing deeply to squelch the urge to run after her, throw her over his shoulder and carry her to his car. He closed his eyes but that just brought to mind her pixie face, pale blue eyes, and kissable lips. Shit. He stood and adjusted himself, then rejoined the party. If his suspicions were true, he might just be meeting his new pack.

His parents were in conversation with Myra and Adam, so he joined them. Myra gave him a considering look.

Uh-oh, best friend inspection time.

"It's definitely different than a forest in New England," Adam was telling Jonas' parents. "But amazing. You can run in canyons, high desert, forest. Some really spectacular land available to us."

"We've been in the city so long," his mom said. "I'm not sure if I'll adjust to the peace and quiet of small-town living."

"Imagine being able to walk out your door and actually smell nature," his dad said. "Instead of people and trash and old food."

"It was an adjustment, for sure," Jonas threw in. "But I think you would like it. And if you change your mind, you change your mind. You're not signing your lives away. And if making the move, changing packs, and retiring all at the same time is too much, maybe keep working for a little while, on your own terms. Cut back, enjoy life." All the things that he had done, that his mother didn't really understand, but would make more sense to them at their stage of life than what they considered appropriate for their thirty-seven-year-old son.

"What do you do?" Myra asked.

"Candace is a dentist, and I'm a high school social studies teacher."

Jonas halfway tuned out of the conversation to watch Cindy chatting with a small group of people by the appetizer table. She was listening to a woman talking animatedly, her hands swinging wildly with whatever story she was telling. Cindy's smile was big and genuine.

"What do you think, Jonas?" his mom asked.

"I think you guys should open a gastropub."

He focused on his parents again, nearly laughed at the shock on their faces. "You've always been foodies, you want some peace and quiet out here, but you also want some of the energy and activity you're used to. It's a small town, so it might not be a huge money maker, but that's not what you're looking for, anyway. You can hire managers and be as involved as you like, and step back when you like."

His mom began telling Myra and Adam about some of her favorites of his dad's recipes, and he turned his attention back to Cindy. She was talking now, but she glanced up, caught his look and gave him a bright smile before looking away again.

He excused himself from the conversation, worked his way

around the room, meeting the others. It was an interesting energy, sort of like a group interview. Everyone trying to put their best foot forward but also reserving judgment on those they met. He noticed that Myra, Adam and Cindy made a point to talk with everyone, and he was curious about what their opinions would be. What were they looking for in new members? Did they have specific goals or were they just open to anyone who wasn't an obvious asshole? It was a fascinating position to be in.

Myra announced that it was time for the run and they all made their way to the backyard. There were several areas set up with sweats for after the run, and room to place your clothes and shoes before the change. He looked around but didn't spot Cindy. He wasn't concerned. He would know her wolf when he found her.

He let the wolf take shape, shaking his whole furry body when the change was complete.

He trotted into the center area, found Myra and Adam greeting the wolves as they approached. His parents came into view, so he greeted them, then went with them to the alpha pair. He'd met his share of alphas over the years, generally respected and liked them. But choosing to live under them was a whole different consideration. When he'd decided to leave New York, he'd visited three packs before meeting Zach in Mountain View. The location had been good, but it was the alpha who had sealed the deal.

A tantalizing scent distracted him, and he knew Cindy had found him. The stunning wolf was gray, like himself, but where his fur stuck to the lighter end of the pallet, hers contained all the gray's imaginable. He offered her muzzle a little lick, received one in return. Then it was time to run.

They chased each other, taking turns being in the lead, playing with the other wolves, but always coming back to each other. The scenery was beautiful, and he guessed that their hosts had selected a route that would show some of the best the area had to offer. It was very different from what he'd known, either in Idaho or New York, somewhat similar to a run he'd gone on when visiting California once.

CHAPTER THREE

All of the visiting wolves had enjoyed a simple breakfast at the pack house before splitting up into groups, some of the wolves going off on their own, some hanging with new friends. Jonas had rented a car for his stay. He spent the morning driving his parents around town so that they could check everything out. They'd explored the library—which hadn't taken long—driven past the schools—there weren't many—and taken a look at the restaurants and bars in the area, as it seemed his idea had taken root for them.

"You're taking Cindy to lunch, but tell me you've arranged something more special than that, Jonas," his mom said as he drove them back to the pack house after their explorations.

"I'd say there is a distinct possibility that she's my mate. Of course I made other plans."

His mom smiled over at him. "I knew I raised you right, I just wanted to be sure you were thinking straight."

"I've got it covered, Mom."

"We chatted with her for a while last night," his dad added.

His look of comic fright had his mom laughing. "Don't scare the boy, Robert."

"I'm not the one who offered to scan his baby photos if she gave you her email address," Robert said. Jonas was pretty sure he wasn't joking. He took a deep breath.

"Mom, if she's my mate, you'll have plenty of years to get to know her, you don't need to spew my life at her in one go."

"Mmm-hmm. What does she do?"

"Candace, let them go on one date before you interrogate him."

"The next time I see him, he might be mated to her!"

"And how will your knowing what she does now have any effect on that?"

"Hmph."

He ignored the banter between his parents and pulled up to the pack house. His mom leaned over and kissed his cheek. "I'm happy for you, honey."

"Thanks, Mom. I'm pretty excited. What are you guys thinking about Alicante? As a pack?"

His mom glanced at his dad and they had one of those silent communications that seemed to last only seconds but conveyed an entire conversation.

"I think we're pretty impressed. I liked Adam and Myra a lot. And if Cindy's settling in here..."

"Yeah, looks like I will be, too. It wouldn't be right to ask her to move to Mountain View when she's having such a good time starting something new here. I like Mountain View, but it won't be that hard to walk away, if I have a mate to walk to."

"You're a good boy." His mom kissed his cheek again. "You go get your girl. Hopefully we won't hear from you until morning."

He smiled, knowing that meant he would be mated in the morning. That was the great thing about being a wolf. It might suck waiting years and years for your mate, but once you had, the dance was short. Though, to be perfectly honest, he was sort of enjoying the dance, was glad they hadn't rushed it last night. Some wolves— the more powerful, like the hierarchy—could barely go hours after meeting without the need to mate overwhelming them. It was kind of nice knowing he had a little time to get to know Cindy, but he hoped at the end of the day, or evening rather, they would be a mated pair.

He followed the directions she'd texted him to her house, trying to be sure he'd thought of everything. He wanted the day to be special for her, wanted her to be completely happy if she was stuck with him. He knew that they wouldn't be mates if they weren't compatible, and everything about her so far made his blood sing and his cock stir. He just wanted to be sure it was the same for her. Well, sort of the same.

Laughing at himself, he pulled up to her house.

CINDY CHECKED HER LIST. Which was silly; she already knew she'd followed every step, without even looking at it. That she'd made it at all was silly, but she'd been nervous and afraid she'd skip something basic. Like brushing her teeth. The list made her a little less anxious.

She put the list back down, then picked it up again and took it to the kitchen. She turned on the stove and lit the paper on fire, turning it around a bit to get the paper really going, then dropped it into the sink. She would have been mortified if Jonas had picked it up and seen her ridiculousness.

She washed the debris down the drain and looked around, making sure everything was picked up. If things went according to plan, Jonas would be moving in.

Sometimes she envied the human process, the dating, the long engagement, the beautiful wedding. Sure, she could have a wedding, but it would just seem kind of frivolous when they were already considered to be married. Sometimes the human mates had them, and she always celebrated with them when they did, but she was a wolf, raised in this culture, and while the idea of it was romantic, so was knowing without a doubt that, if she found her mate, she would have a partner for life.

She wouldn't trade that certainty for anything. But why had she told him they should take the slow route? What had she been thinking? If they'd had sex last night, they would know for sure they were mates and be starting the rest of their lives, right now.

Deep breaths. She checked her watch. Five more minutes. Maybe she should just drag him into the house and be done with it, rather than taking him to the restaurant as she had planned.

Her ears perked when she heard a car approaching. She checked out the window, thrilled to see him in the driver's seat. Early was good. She opened the door and watched him come toward her. He was wearing nice jeans and a long-sleeved shirt that showed off his fabulous chest without quite looking like he was intentionally showing off his fabulous chest. She approved.

Butterflies danced in her stomach and she felt a little dizzy, but then she realized that was because she wasn't breathing. She pulled in a lungful, just in time, because he strode right to her and kissed her. Kissed her hard and long and perfect, his arms tight around her, his delicious smell enveloping her, his hard body supporting her.

She didn't know how long it lasted, whined a little when he pulled back.

"Public. If you want to wait, we need to get out in public."

She debated. Hard.

His lips quirked at her indecision. "We have the rest of our lives to be mates. I want that, with you. I can hardly wait to start that. But we only have a little bit of time left to be two people getting to know each other." He pulled back, offered her a hand.

She knew she could change his mind in a heartbeat. Remembered it had been her decision first. He was right. They would have forever together as mates, but only today as two wolves getting to know each other without the connection of being mated.

While she wanted that forever, more than anything, knowing it was coming helped her ease back, take his hand, and follow him to the car. She would enjoy this time of getting to know him just for himself. Then she would jump his bones and confirm what she already knew.

They were meant for each other, and would be bonded in a way that they would only ever know with each other.

He followed her directions to the nearby town of Silver City, and the diner she'd selected. It was on her list of restaurants to try. There were plenty of empty tables, so they were seated immediately. He held her chair for her, resting his hand on her shoulder for just a second. It had the odd effect of steadying her and heating her up at the same time.

"Tell me about what you do," he invited.

She told him about her blog, how it had grown from something of a hobby to a full-time business that she loved. He was attentive, asking good questions to show he was listening and interested, but not talking over her. She almost didn't order dessert, but he promised they would be using up a lot of calories soon, and needed the extra energy. From some, it might have come out creepy or smarmy. From the man she found herself tangling fingers with as they talked, she found it sexy as hell. She ordered a hot fudge sundae and he ordered a slice of apple pie.

"I can't believe we spent that whole time talking about me and my job," she said as they walked back to the car. "It's your turn."

"Okay, but first tell me how I'm doing." His voice was teasing as he led her to the passenger door and reached for it. She blocked him, leaning against the car, and pulled him close to her with her hands fisted in his shirt.

"Well, you listened without talking over me. You didn't dominate the conversation but you also didn't leave it all up to me, you were polite to the server but didn't ogle her even though she was quite pretty, you didn't talk with your mouth full even once, and you fought me over going halfsies on the check, but managed to do so in a charming way."

He laughed. "Is that your full first-date checklist, or is there more?"

"It would be cheating to tell you that, but since you're scoring pretty high so far, I'd say you shouldn't be too worried."

His teasing smiled faded to serious. "I want you to be happy about this."

She cupped his cheek, leaned up on her tiptoes. "Every minute we've been together I've gotten happier and happier. I can't wait for you to feel that for yourself."

He groaned and kissed her, teasing her with soft, light kisses when she'd expected hard and fast. She spread her hands on his chest, enjoyed the feeling of his muscles contracting as he kissed her. She wanted more. Wanted him. No more waiting.

"Take me home," she urged.

Another groan as he pulled back, as though it was the last thing he wanted to do. "I want to take you somewhere. It's not too far, about a forty-five-minute drive."

She blinked. She'd assumed they would just go back to her house and…well, make things happen. "You want to go somewhere other than my house?"

"I want this to be special. I'll drive fast. But not too fast," he added quickly.

She laughed and shook her head. "Okay, if that's what you want. But we don't have to."

"I think it will be worth it. We'll swing by your place and you can pack an overnight bag."

She got in the car, on the one hand disappointed that they would have to wait a bit longer, but on the other hand, absurdly pleased that he was making an effort to make the occasion extra special. She'd asked him for the slow road, and he was giving her just that, but making her want him more and more.

The trip back to her house was quick and she suggested he wait in the car while she grabbed her things. Now that she was committed to waiting, she liked the idea, wanted to see what he had planned out for them. But was worried that if he came into the house with her, she'd get impatient and jump him.

He agreed, looked like he was going to pull her into a kiss, then thought better of it.

Giggling, she got out of the car and practically ran for the door. It only took five minutes to use the bathroom to freshen up, throw her toothbrush, toothpaste, deodorant, hairbrush and makeup bag into a tote. She added a change of clothes and the sexy underwear set she'd bought online a couple of years ago and only worn once. It had been her fourth date with a guy, and they'd ended up arguing and breaking up before the evening ended, so he hadn't even seen the lingerie.

He pointedly glanced at his watch when she threw the bag in the backseat and got into the car, but she knew he was teasing. "Well, it took me a while to pick between all my lingerie and find just the right thing."

His hand went to his heart and his head flopped back on the rest. "I totally asked for that."

"You did. Now drive, James!" She pointed forward. Which was silly, because forward was her house. But he got the idea and reversed out of her drive.

"Alright, so we have drive time, tell me about you."

"I grew up in New York. You met my parents, good people."

"I had a nice chat with them. Your mom is cute and your dad is funny."

He looked over at her, blinked slowly.

She laughed. "No, really."

"Right. Sure. So, anyway, I started out at a recruiting firm, then started my own agency."

"So, helping people find good jobs?"

"Yes, mostly executive level. And the other way around, helping companies find the right person for the job."

"Did you like it?"

"I did, for a long time. It was stressful, going out on my own, but I enjoyed the fast pace, and I really liked helping companies, and individuals, find the right fit. But I started to burn out. The money was good, but I couldn't keep up the pace forever. When I found myself sort of encouraging people into a position just to get the assignment filled, I realized I'd hit my limit. I could have backed off, found a partner, hired a manager, something, but I decided I wanted a clean break. So I sold the company."

"And you moved to Idaho."

"Right. About three years ago, I took a bit of a vacation, traveled to several cities, met up with several packs, and decided Zach and Mountain View were a good fit. And they have been, I've enjoyed my time there. As for work, they needed a bartender to work a certain shift at the bar, and I needed something to do while I decided what I wanted to do, if that makes sense."

"Perfectly. Especially if you had enough money from selling your company that you didn't need to make major plans right away. The freedom to be patient."

"Exactly. Although some—my parents—might argue three years is too long. I just haven't felt the need to launch into anything more substantial yet."

She had the sudden realization that he'd picked Mountain View as his home not too long ago, and may have no desire to move. He had come to New Mexico to help his parents, after all, not because he was interested in joining a new pack.

"You're happy in Idaho, then?" she asked.

She must not have succeeded in keeping the nerves out of her voice, because he reached over and took her hand.

"Happy, yes. Tied down, no. Unwilling to move on, no."

The boulder that had sprung up from nowhere to reside in her belly suddenly dissolved. And with it, so did the certainty that she had to be part of this new pack. While she was enjoying the novelty of helping a pack grow from scratch, it wasn't more important than the happiness of her mate. If he *was* her mate, that was. It was a relief, knowing that she would happily move if that was what was important to him, and he seemed willing to do the same.

"Well, we can figure that out later, the possibilities are endless," she said.

He raised her hand to his lips and kissed it.

"Okay, then. You moved to Idaho three years ago, and you've been sort of treading water. Haven't decided on what the next phase of your life is going to bring you."

"I guess maybe I was waiting for now." He looked at her, and the sheer hope in his expression mirrored her own. She was nearly one hundred percent positive that he was her mate. Soon they would know for sure—and she would never be alone again. She would have a partner, and she could hardly wait. She was still slightly nervous, though she couldn't really even say why. She needed to distract herself.

"Do you think your parents might really open a restaurant?" she asked.

"I think it would be great for them. They're ready to retire, but mostly because they've been doing the same things forever, not because they're too old to work. If they go forward, I'll encourage them to get a good manager so that it's not all on them. It can be a hell of a lot of work, but they have the money to do it right and not exhaust themselves with it."

"The pack would certainly support the business, but new restaurants are a hard go in big cities, I'm not sure how successful they would be in such a small town."

"There are a lot of things to consider, and maybe they'll think of something totally different they might want to do, now that I've nudged them outside the box a bit. They've always been very good with their finances, so that's something they don't have to worry about as long as they don't go crazy. Everything else is just icing on the cake, as far as I'm concerned."

"That's great. I have no idea how my parents' finances are, isn't that terrible?"

"Not everyone is comfortable talking about it, which is sad, I think." He glanced over at her. "We can talk about it."

"Absolutely. But...after, okay? It sounds like you're in good shape, and I'm in good shape, so let's just be sure this is what we know it is, then we can get down to the details of money and location and jobs and stuff."

"Yes, ma'am."

"Oh, shoot, I forgot to pack my paddle."

"Don't worry, I packed mine."

She tried not to laugh, to tease him more, but couldn't quite manage it. Giving up, she leaned back. "Are we there yet?"

"Five more minutes."

Smiling, she enjoyed the easy silence as they ate up the miles. When she saw a sign advertising private resort cabins, she guessed that was their destination, but didn't ask. After another fifteen minutes, he followed the signs and exited the highway.

Before long they were passing cabins with little wood signs that said Acacia, Bergamot, Crag Lily, Dragonhead and Everlasting Pea.

"We've got the end unit," he explained, turning at a sign that read "Fairy Bells".

"I'm kind of curious where they would have gone with the G. I think they need another cabin," she said.

He snorted and pulled to a stop. The cabin wasn't big, was made with real logs, and sported colorful flowers under the window. She got out of the car and grabbed her bag as he did the same. He waited for her at the front of the car and held out his hand. She took it with a smile, no longer nervous, just excited.

Well, okay, maybe a tiny bit nervous. What if this was just strong attraction and wishful thinking and they would both be horribly disappointed at the end of it?

Giving her a tiny yank, he met her eyes as she moved toward him. "It's going to be good. Actually, I'm pretty sure it will be amazing."

She pulled in a deep breath. "I know. I do. I'm just a little nervous that it's all too easy."

"We've waited a long time for this," he reminded her.

"You're right. Let's stop waiting. I want to start the rest of my life. Here. Now."

"That's my girl." He pulled her in for a kiss. She melted into him, her face tipped up to meet his lips. Apparently he was tired of bending over to meet her, because he picked her up, slipping his arms under her butt to support her. She squeaked, wrapped her legs around his hips, but didn't let go of the kiss.

He turned and walked to the cabin and she finally pulled free with a laugh. "You need to watch where we're going!"

"Yes, ma'am."

On the porch, he looked around, then moved a ceramic frog so that he could pick up the key that was underneath. He managed to open the door without dropping her or his bag, and she managed to hang on without bumping him with *her* bag. Too much.

When they were inside, he let her slide down and they turned to take a look. The cabin was rustic, probably decorated in the late eighties, but it was clean, charming, and had a fireplace and tiny kitchen. Large windows took up most of the far wall, and they walked over to see a spectacular view of the Gila National Forest. He wrapped an arm around her shoulder and she snuggled in.

"It's beautiful. Thank you for doing this."

He pulled out his phone and worked the screen. "Let's dance." The first strains of one of her favorite songs, "Stand By Me", came from the phone. He set it on the table and she turned into his arms. She wouldn't have guessed him to be a dancer. Honestly, she wasn't much of one herself, but held in his arms, mostly just swaying to the music, her heart tripped over into love.

JONAS HELD Cindy in his arms, dancing—if you could call it that—to the old song. He was on the edge of peaceful happiness and needy anticipation. He wanted the night to go on forever, but he wanted her to be his. Wanted to be hers, so she would never question their place together. Wanted to be inside of her and on top of her and underneath her and…well. He wanted her.

As the song neared the end, he pushed her out a little, gave her a bit of a spin. The next song started, and he waited a heartbeat to see her reaction, a little nervous about his gamble.

The distinctive first chords of Marvin Gaye's "Let's Get it On" cut into the room.

Little lines appeared in her forehead as the lyrics began, and then she began to laugh. And laugh. Until she was doubled-over with it.

How could he resist her? She was made for him. He scooped her up, holding tight as she was shaking with laughter. Her arms wrapped around him to hold on and she buried her face in his neck.

He picked up the phone and carried her to the bedroom. There was little else in the small room besides a queen bed and a dresser with fresh flowers on top. That was more than he needed. He tossed her on the bed so that she bounced, and turned off the phone, cutting poor Marvin off mid-lyric. He set the phone on the dresser and advanced on the bed.

She watched him coming, and he liked seeing the anticipation on her face, the desire. But there was also a touch of nerves.

He could relate. Chances were very strong that they were about to be mated, and more than anything, he wanted to make her happy with the choice that had been made for them.

Intellectually, he knew they would both be happy. Hell, he already was.

Actually, now that it was coming down to it, what would he do if she turned out *not* to be his mate? Could he really be that attached to her already that the idea he was wrong about her being his mate could cause that stab to the gut?

"What are you thinking," she asked.

He realized he'd been staring at her. He swallowed. "I want this to be right. For you. And I want you to be my mate. I'm going to be really, really pissed if you're not."

The pleased smile that blossomed across her face made his nerves worthwhile. She crooked a finger at him. "Come here. Let's make it right."

He put one hand on her ankle, dragged her a bit closer, and pulled off her shoe. Then the other. She sat up and grabbed the hem of her top.

"Wait," he said. "Let me."

She let go, took his offered hand and slid off the bed to stand in front of him. He cupped her face and tasted her soft, inviting lips. Her hands settled on his hips and her lips opened in welcome. He kissed her, softly, slowly, moving one hand to the nape of her neck, the other sliding down to her lower back, pulling her in close. Tight. When her hands began to roam his back, pulling him, fisting in his shirt, he broke the kiss and teased her jaw with his nose. "You taste so sweet. So perfect," he murmured in her ear.

"I want more," she begged. She yanked at his shirt.

"Patience."

"Why?"

He laughed. "I don't know, seems like a good idea to me."

"Maybe I disagree—"

She broke off with a gasp when he nipped the side of her neck, nibbled lightly down her shoulder. Her whole body shivered, and he nudged her sweater out of the way, enjoying her sensitivity. Her fingers were back to clasping at his shirt as he teased the curve of her shoulder with nips and licks and kisses.

"Jonas," she panted.

"Cynthia," he answered, not changing his pace but moving his hand to cup her ass and press her center more tightly to his dick.

Her head fell back with a little gasp when he sucked gently on the sensitive spot he'd found. Fuck, she tasted so good. Sweet and salty, eager and hot. He was going to bite her, right here, when the mating bond hit them.

And he knew it would. It had to. Because he wasn't going to give her up.

Kissing the marked spot, he moved back, pulled her sweater up. She helped, laughing with him when their arms tangled and the sweater got wrapped around her head. Finally she was free, and he couldn't resist her laughing mouth, went back for more.

She accepted his kiss, but her hands moved to his front and unclasped his buckle. The leather slid out of the belt loops, and she moved on to the button of his jeans. Breaking free of the kiss, he left her to the task and focused on the pretty lilac lace bra in front of him. It cupped her breasts nicely, enticingly. He traced the lace with one finger, ever so gently. She shivered, but her fingers dove into his jeans and tested his length.

She didn't have much room to work, though, so he was pretty

confident he would win this round. He shaped the lace cups with his palms, hefting the small weight of her breasts. He thumbed her nipples through the lace, encouraging them to tight peaks. His mouth watered. "Unhook your bra," he told her, giving her breasts another squeeze.

She whimpered. "You do it, I'm busy here." Pulling her hand free of his pants, she tried to shove them down his hips. He pushed against her, keeping the pants pinned. Her growl of frustration made him smile. He tickled the valley between her breasts with his nose, all the while giving little squeezes of his handful. She gave up her efforts with his jeans and speared her fingers into his hair, trying to guide his mouth to her nipple.

"The bra," he reminded her between licks and nips.

She growled again, but complied, reaching her arms behind her to work the clasp. When the ends fell free, he let the pretty fabric fall and reshaped her breasts with his palms, then let her demanding hands guide him to her straining nipple. He pulled it between his lips, sucked hard, while lightly pinching and pulling the other. Her breath quickened and her fingers tightened in his hair. She arched her back, offering more of herself. He backed her against the bed, hitched her up and lay her back. Giving her plump nipple a last lick, he went to work on the other.

"Oh, fuck, that's so good," she moaned. "I want you naked, though." She tugged his hair. "Please, Jonas."

He gave one lingering pull before moving back. Watching her glazed, hungry expression was the best aphrodisiac he'd ever experienced. He kicked off his shoes and shoved his pants and boxers down. She licked her lips. He groaned and reached for her. "You are so beautiful." He ran his hands along her thighs, her hips, her waist. Straddled her and dropped down slowly until he was lying along her length, careful to hold his weight off her. He slipped one arm underneath her and flipped.

Her gasp ended on a laugh as they came to a stop with her on top. She propped her hands on his chest and let the laugh fade away as they stared at each other.

He brought his hand to her face, cupped her cheek. Wasn't sure if the tremble was on her side or his. Didn't care. "Thank god I found you."

She smiled, and he knew he would always remember the beauty of this moment.

"Make me yours, Jonas. I need you to be mine."

"Yes, ma'am."

He held her hips as she moved her legs up, straddling him. Her hair flopped over her face when she looked down to study him, trace her fingers along his length. He didn't push, didn't urge her on, just moved her hair out of her face so he could watch as she fisted him.

She lifted up, came down over him slowly, one torturous inch at a time, a little swirl, and then she was seated. She braced her hand on his chest and finally looked back up at him.

Her eyes grew wide, which he totally understood—as he could feel her soul mating with his. It went from a tiny vibration to a full tingle before settling down into a sweet awareness.

"Wow," she breathed.

"Yeah. *Really* wow."

A tear rolled down her cheek, and he wiped it away with his thumb without breaking eye contact.

"You are so mine, now."

Another tear. "Not as much as you're mine."

"Totally as much. But that works for me."

"Yeah, that works." She glanced down at where their bodies were joined. "I'm going to rock your world now."

"Me first." He didn't give her a chance to react, just wrapped his arm around her and rolled again, landing on top of her. His mouth met hers, his hips pumping in time with his tongue. Her nails scratched at his back, her heels hooking around his legs, pulling him close, giving them both leverage.

She broke the kiss to cry out, and he took the opportunity to nuzzle her neck, find the sweet spot, and bite down.

Her scream was long, as was the orgasm that squeezed around

him so tightly, it took everything he had not to let go. He wanted more.

He licked the bite mark, pulled her earlobe between his teeth, giving it a little nip. Her lax legs twitched. He nibbled along her jaw, teased her lips until she gave him her tongue. Then he began to move again. Her legs wrapped around him once more, his thrusts slow and easy until she began to moan again. He resumed his earlier pace, snuck a hand down to rub her clit with his thumb, slow, deliberate circles that had a tiny little whine escaping her throat.

Pulling free of the kiss, he arched his back, changing his angle slightly. Her whole body went rigid, and she called out his name. He buried his face in her neck and came as hard as he could ever remember coming.

He rolled to the side enough not to crush her and collapsed onto the bed. She snuggled in next to him, and he managed the energy to sift her hair through his fingers, enjoying the way the soft strands fell back into place while their breathing evened out.

"That was worth the wait, I suppose," she said, the tease in her voice making him smile.

"Yeah, I'd say so. Even better knowing we have about a billion more chances to perfect it."

She snorted. "If that's *not* perfect, I'm not sure I'll be able to survive perfect."

"*You* are perfect."

"Heh, wait until you see me spend an hour setting up the perfect shot for some food or freaking out because I can't find the exact shade of purple that I need for something."

"Stop being cute, you're just turning me on again."

"And that's a problem, because...?" She moved over him, resting her arms on his chest and her chin on her arms.

"Oh, right, totally not a problem."

She smiled. "This is kind of amazing."

He smoothed a piece of hair and hooked it behind her ear. "Totally amazing. I mean, you know what it's going to be like, in theory. You see it in others. But *holy shit*."

"Exactly." She sighed, seeming content. "Thanks, by the way. For setting up this cabin. It's really sweet."

"My pleasure. It was fun exploring online to see what's around here that we can check out, assuming the pack stays."

"You want to move here?" she asked. "Because I'm willing to move to Idaho if you want to stay there."

"You would do that? After working so hard to get things set up here?" Deeply touched, he watched her intently, saw nothing but acceptance.

"Absolutely. If it's important to you, it's important to me. I needed a change, and moving to Alicante was what worked for me at the time. And it brought us together. I would love to stay and be a part of this pack, but it's not something that I would put above your happiness."

He lifted his head to kiss her, deep and hard. When he finally pulled free, her eyes shone brightly.

"I want to stay here," he said. "I like Myra and Adam. I like the idea of being on the ground floor of a new pack. How often does that chance come up?"

"Hardly ever."

"Hardly ever. So we're agreed?"

"Absolutely. Shall we go watch the sunset from the porch?"

"Perfect."

SHE GRABBED her bag and went to the bathroom, and he pulled on his jeans and picked up the soft blanket that had fallen off the end of the bed. He went into the main room of the cabin and found a bottle of wine, an opener and two glasses on the kitchen counter, as he'd requested. Making short work of the cork, he had two glasses poured by the time Cindy wandered out.

She'd switched from her jeans to tight leggings and a longer sweater. The neck was wide enough that he could see the red mark on her shoulder. Deep satisfaction washed through him. She was

41

beautiful—and she was his. He couldn't wait to get to know her better.

She accepted the glass he offered and led the way to the porch. A small glider with a cushion was perfectly positioned to watch the sunset. He handed his glass to her and spread the blanket behind their shoulders, curling it and his arm around her so they were close. She returned his drink to him and he propped his feet up on the railing, feeling a contentment that he'd never even realized he was missing.

"This is lovely," she said.

Somehow he knew she meant more than the cabin, the glider, the view. "Yeah. It's probably a good thing we didn't realize how amazing it would be, or the wait would have felt torturous."

"Seriously. Some mates are so lucky to find each other early on. But then again, I kind of like this version of me that you're meeting. I mean, I liked me at twenty, too, but…"

"I know what you mean. On the one hand it would have been nice reaching this stage of the journey together, but on the other hand, there's satisfaction in having become this person, someone I'm proud of enough to be your mate."

She curled into him, her legs underneath her, her head on his shoulder. "You totally get me."

He smiled and kissed her head. They watched a couple of birds chase each other in silence for a while before he prodded her into conversation.

"You met my parents. I'm an only child. What about your family?"

"My parents, my brother Bill, his wife Juanita, and their two kids, Danny and Sara, live in Texas. Bill and I get along great, and I love Juanita and the kids. I visit at least once a year. My relationship with my parents is kind of weird. We sort of tolerate each other. I can't really explain why. I actually found out that my mom was assuming I would move back there eventually, but I honestly have never considered it."

"Any particular reason? Other than the thing with your parents?" Which he figured he'd save questions about for another day.

"Not really. I started looking for a new job because my boss was someone I couldn't really respect, and she was our fourth. Once I started looking outside the pack, outside the state, and realized I could go anywhere I wanted, I never looked back."

"What was it about her that you didn't like?"

"She wasn't a good manager, made decisions that I thought were kind of sketchy, and while that didn't have anything to do with the pack, it's a difficult thing when you don't respect your hierarchy."

"I imagine so."

"I worked for her for several months, then started looking for another job, and the rest is history. I loved St. Louis as soon as I visited, but I wasn't sure how permanent it would be. You can like a pack when you first meet, but you can't really know until you're there a while, you know?"

"Definitely. The first impression is important, but not always the whole story. And things change. All packs have an ebb and flow, a reshuffling as the hierarchy changes, families grow, mates happen. It's healthy not to feel you have to live and die with one pack."

"I think a lot of people do feel that way. It might be part of what was wrong in Arizona. Myra hasn't told me anything more than she's made public, I just think that for the legitimate pack to have let the rogue pack exist, the members must have never felt they could go to National and get help, or even just move to somewhere more healthy. There had to be a feeling that they couldn't leave." She shook her head. "I'm making assumptions."

"Maybe. It's plausible. But if any of the original Arizona members end up in our pack, it wouldn't hurt to keep an eye on the pulse of the pack, make sure it feels inclusive without being oppressive."

"Yeah, you totally get me." She lifted her head up to him and he kissed her lips. She tasted of red wine and promises of the future.

Geez, find a mate and he suddenly turned into a romantic fool. Funny how that didn't bother him at all.

CHAPTER FOUR

Cindy snuggled in even closer to Jonas as they watched the sun sink to the horizon.

"Anyway, as it turned out, my first impression was spot on and St. Louis was a great pack. Happy and healthy, a good mix of young and old, ambitious and stable, serious and carefree."

"Most people don't give that much thought to what makes a good pack cohesive," he said, sounding impressed.

She shrugged. "My blog is called *This Layered Life*. It's about acknowledging and understanding the different layers we live with. Like, sometimes you come to the blog for a nice recipe, for an article about xeriscaping your lawn, or how to find a great hairdresser. That's one layer, and it's totally valid and necessary. But there's more, right? There's always another layer. Like, while you're planning that Pinterest-style party for your three-year-old, are you budgeting for the basic bills, plus Christmas, plus the down payment on your starter home? If you don't have enough to save for both right now, is it better to prioritize your retirement savings or your kid's college education? If you hate your job, is it better to look for another one, consider going into business for yourself, or even consider some ways to make your current job better."

"Wow. I'm impressed."

"Oh, please, to have been halfway decent at your job, you must have been pretty good at looking beneath the surface. To find the right person for the right position, rather than just slotting people in where it was easy." She poked his chest. "Go ahead, tell me I'm wrong."

He laughed. "My woman is smart. This pleases me."

"Hmph," she said, but she was smiling. They held the silence for a bit as the sun finally dropped past the horizon in a glorious display that set the wispy clouds on fire. "I could definitely get used to the desert," she whispered. "Remind me to add this place to my list of possible job opportunities for new wolves. The drive isn't bad."

"You have a list?" he asked.

"I have a lot of lists. I'm a fan of lists."

His lips quirked. "Do you have a list of good qualities in a mate?"

She leaned back, ran her gaze slowly up and down his body, pursed her lips. "No, of course not."

He threw his head back and laughed, dragging her back into his side, squeezing her tight. She smiled, enjoying the sound as his body shook beneath her. She put her hand on his abdomen to feel the muscles tighten and decided his bare skin was worth some more exploration than she'd managed so far. Sitting up, she rose to her knees and swung one leg over, plopped down into his lap, her hands braced on his shoulders.

***

"WELL, HELLO THERE."

"Mmm," she murmured, squeezing his shoulders then moving her hands down along his arms. His biceps bunched as she passed over them, and she giggled. His hands cupped her hips, then slid around to her butt and gave a little squeeze. She ran the backs of her fingers up his abs like they were truly a washboard, then pinched his nipples lightly.

He drew in a breath, tightened his grip on her glutes, his thumbs taking up a little caress. She leaned in close to his face, bypassed his lips and cruised along his jaw, nipping and tasting until she reached his earlobe. It wasn't detached, like hers, and she wondered if their kids would follow her genes or his. A small thrill shot through her at the idea of their babies.

She nuzzled the hollow behind his ear, drew in a deep breath. The smell of Jonas, her mate, made her giddy.

One of the things she'd always thought was nice about being a werewolf was knowing exactly where she was in her cycle, when she was fertile. Now wasn't her time, so they didn't have to have a conversation about condoms, didn't need to interrupt the moment. But she made a mental note to see what page he was on. Somehow she wasn't worried that they'd be of vastly different opinions on the subject of children.

She ran her nails lightly down his chest, then harder. When he started to move his hands, she murmured, "Not yet." He stilled, and she opened the button of his jeans, lowered the zipper. He hadn't bothered to put his boxers back on, so she gently pulled him free, explored with her fingers before gripping him tightly. "So very nice."

He swallowed loud enough for her to hear before answering. "I'm glad you approve."

She smiled. "Oh, yeah." She rose up, his hands automatically helping her keep balance as she shimmied her pants down, lifted one leg to free it, then the other. When she was sufficiently naked, she angled herself over him. He shifted farther down the seat and gave her just what she needed. She dropped, slowly but steadily, filling herself with his hard length. She met his eyes, the incredible heat and passion in them made her wetter, so she dropped the last bit with a groan.

"Fuck, baby."

He stood, causing her to squeak, though she was safely banded in his arms. Her legs wrapped tightly around his hips as he turned them, put her back against the cabin.

"Okay?" he asked.

She nodded, threaded her fingers through his hair, clenched tight.

He groaned and leaned forward, pulling her nipple into his mouth, swirling his tongue deliciously. She closed her eyes and leaned her head back against the wall as he began to move. In and out, suck and swirl, his powerful body making her melt in all the best ways. She heard herself calling his name, a bare whisper all she could manage, as he pushed her closer and closer to the edge of release.

Switching to her other breast, he pulled strongly with his teeth. Her cry rang out in the dark but she knew there was no one close enough to hear.

"Come for me," he growled. He slammed up into her, and she did as he demanded. It took all her strength to keep her legs tight around him as he slowed, but continued to move, riding her orgasm until he, too, threw his head back and shouted his release.

She let him support her as her legs dropped, and then he swiftly picked her up in his arms. "Be careful," she teased. "If you keep being this sexy, I might swoon."

He kissed the tease right out of her and sat back down on the glider, somehow managing to wrap them back up in the blanket. She lay against him as their breathing evened out, sleepily satisfied with her day.

"I WAS THINKING we should go for a run together, but I don't think I want to get up anytime soon," she told him.

"We can go for a dawn run. The start of our new lives together."

"Damn, you're so good. I'm sold on that, even though I am *not* a morning person."

He put on a shocked face. "What? Finally I find something imperfect about you?"

She gave him a fake glower. "You're a morning person?"

"I'm so totally not," he answered, deadpan.

Laughing, she smacked his chest lightly. "What would you have done if I was?"

"Enjoyed already-brewed coffee when I got up in the morning?"

"Heh. Yeah, probably. Now the coffee will be your job."

"I can handle that."

"Have you thought about what you want to do here? With your days, I mean."

"Not really, not yet. I want to get a better feel for the place, for the pack. After I get a few good feels of my mate."

She smiled, enjoying him immensely.

"I wonder how the others are doing. How many are hoping to stay and how many are already on their way back home."

"Do you need to check in with anybody for your work?"

"Nah, it can all wait until tomorrow. One of the beautiful things about being the boss, although I can be more demanding on myself than others."

"I'll help keep you in line."

"Yeah, right, that will be interesting to see."

"If I think you're overdoing it, I'll just wander around the house naked."

"Hmm, you may have a workable strategy there, I'm not gonna lie."

They made their way back into the cabin when the light had fully gone. She switched on a lamp while he lit a fire under the wood already prepared in the fireplace. She poured them more wine and looked in the fridge. There were two steaks marinating in a dish and a bowl of green beans, already trimmed. She found garlic, spices, olive oil and sliced almonds.

"I really like this place. Do they do this for everyone or did you make specific instructions?"

"I made specific instructions, but they seemed prepared for the requests."

They worked together as if they'd done it a hundred times, this time using her phone for music. He sang along to several of the songs, so she figured they had at least some compatibility in that department. Hell, it seemed they had compatibility in every department. She'd known, believed in, the magic of a mate, but had never comprehended the true perfection and beauty of it.

"You know, Myra had a mate before Adam."

Jonas paused in his task of stirring the sautéing beans. "Seriously?"

"Yeah, he died before I moved out there. I think they were together for two or three years."

"Holy shit."

"Sorry, I didn't mean to bring this down. I just was thinking how amazing it is, and I always knew it was awful for her to lose her mate, but now—"

He put the wooden spoon down and drew her into his arms. "I know, baby. I can't imagine. Don't want to imagine it. I'm glad she's got Adam, now."

"Me, too." She reached up to give him a kiss. "I'm okay, don't let the beans burn. I'm just...happy. And that made me sad," she laughed. "But I'll go back to being happy."

"I'm happy, too. I knew I would be. But this...this is indescribable."

She turned the steaks and searched out the plates. He lit the candles already waiting on the table and poured the last of the wine into their glasses. She plated the beans and topped them with the almond slivers while he pulled the steaks to rest. When they had everything together and sat, he offered his glass in a toast. Touched, she held hers up.

"To our forever."

Her throat got so tight she couldn't say anything for a long moment. "To our forever," she managed to repeat. She took a tiny sip then met him for a kiss. Long and slow, just like their first date. The idea made her giggle, and she pulled back, waggled her eyebrows at him.

"Fuel up, big man."

Grinning at her, he took a large bite.

CHAPTER FIVE

Since neither of them were morning people, Jonas was surprised that they *did* wake up early enough to go for a morning run at dawn. Her naked body wrapped around his had him re-thinking the plan, but she gave him a cheeky grin and climbed out of bed. He was mesmerized by the view as she stretched up on tiptoes, arms pulled tight over her head. Then she transformed and led the way out of the room to the cabin door.

He opened it up and pulled it closed behind them, before calling on his wolf. He wouldn't have thought it possible for the intensity of his feelings for his mate, for the bond that had formed so solidly, to increase, but when they touched as wolves, muzzle to muzzle, her scent filling him up, he was nearly overwhelmed. She licked at him and twined her body around his, marking him with her scent.

They ran and explored, keeping wide of the cabins, encountering some birds and small game. Eventually they hunted and rested, and it was early afternoon before they made it back to the cabin. When they'd gathered their things and closed up the cabin, he decided it would be nice to come back for their anniversary. By the time they were reaching the outskirts of Alicante, it was nearly dusk.

"If you feel like it, I can show you some land I scoped out and thought might be good for a house," Cindy said, her fingers idly playing with his where they rested on her thigh. "It's on the way back to the house. I wasn't sold on it, want to look around some more, but it will catch you up to where I am on the search. Or we can go look another day."

"Build a brand-new house?" he asked. "I've never done that. Kind of like building the new pack? From the ground up?"

"I hadn't really thought about it like that. I just hadn't seen much that I liked for long-term, when I was looking for a place to move into. Do you think it would be too much work? Contractors and house plans and all of that?"

He glanced over, saw her thoughtful frown. "A lot of work, sure. But probably not too much. Could be kind of fun."

"There would be a lot of lists," she warned him, her frown turning into a grin. "Lots and lots of lists."

"I think I can handle that." He followed her directions and pulled the car over. When he got out, he drew in a deep breath, considering. She grabbed his hand and tugged him along, pointing out the boundaries, the possible views, depending on where the house went up, her enthusiasm contagious. He could see it, could feel it, could imagine making a home that was totally theirs. Putting his arms around her, he held her tight as he saw their future stretching out before them, the rightness of it all settling deep into his bones.

Cindy hugged him just as tightly, then turned in his arms to look at the view that could be theirs. "Ideally, I'd like to be closer to the pack house, if that becomes permanent."

"And something a little less flat," he added. "Like you said, this is good, workable, but I wouldn't mind seeing more options. It gives me ideas about what could be."

When they got back to the car, he asked her where she wanted to go first. "Home? Adam and Myra's? My parents'? A restaurant for dinner?"

"Your parents. Then I'll call my parents. Then we'll take yours out to dinner."

"Will you want to go see your parents? Your brother?"

"At some point. And it's possible they'll want to come out here. It's hard to say."

"Then we'll play it by ear."

His mom cried when she hugged Cindy, and his dad sounded a little choked up as he congratulated them both. Her parents said the right things, though her mother was clearly reserving judgment until they met, and her father hadn't been terribly impressed when told Jonas was currently working as a bartender.

When they'd settled in at the restaurant and ordered their food, Cindy asked his parents if they'd made a decision on the new pack.

"We're definitely interested. And Myra and Adam seem receptive, although I suppose we won't really know until we officially petition to join." His mom frowned at the uncertainty. "Cindy, do you know if they'll be making decisions right away, or if they're waiting to see how many people request to join?"

"I don't think they plan on waiting. While there's some filling-of-slots type of decisions, as far as hierarchy and security, for the most part they're more interested in finding the right fit for both sides. They don't feel the need to start off big, but there's also no reason to keep real small, if there are plenty of people who do want to join."

"That's good," his dad said. "I think that's good. And smart."

His mom nodded approvingly.

"Have you guys given more thought to what you would want to do if you move here?" he asked.

"A bit, but your mom and I don't feel the need to rush into a decision. We can take our time, get ourselves settled, then see what appeals. By then, with the pack getting settled as well, different opportunities might occur to us that we wouldn't even see right now."

"Also smart," Cindy said, as the waiter brought their plates.

"Tell us about what you do, dear."

Cindy spent the meal stealing bites between answering questions about her work. A lifestyle blog was not something his parents understood without lots of explanation, but she was patient and amusing, telling them examples of the kinds of articles she posted. He interjected enough to make sure she had time to actually eat her food.

They skipped dessert and headed to the pack house, after dropping his parents off. Cindy drove so that he could call Zach and Hillary and give them the news. The alpha pair was very excited for him. Though sad to hear that he would be moving, they completely understood.

As soon as they reached the front porch, the door flew open and Myra pulled Cindy into the house with a squeal and wrapped her up in a hug.

Adam was holding a bottle of champagne. "Congratulations," he said, popping the cork and moving to the glasses that had been set on a nearby table.

"Tell me you're staying," Myra blurted out. "I'm happy for you either way, but I'll be extra, super happy if you tell me you're staying."

Adam cleared his throat. "But no pressure. You need to do what's best for you as a couple."

"Right. That," Myra said as she handed them each a filled glass.

Cindy laughed and gave her friend another quick hug. "I won't leave you in suspense. We're staying."

"Then we're extra, super happy for you, and for us. Welcome to the pack, Jonas."

"Thank you, I'm glad to be here. Mostly because being here brought me Cindy, but I've been liking what I'm seeing with the pack, as well. I'm honored to be part of the new adventure."

They all drank, and then Myra and Adam officially welcomed him into the pack bonds. It was an odd sensation, being part of such a small group. With just four of them, and with his bond to Cindy being so intense, it was a much deeper feeling than the one he'd had with Mountain View.

He looked at his mate, smiling at her best friend as she sipped her wine. They had a rental and might consider buying land and building a house, but all of that was inconsequential. He was home.

Six weeks later

Jonas carefully lowered his end of the sofa to the hardwood floor, keeping pace with Adam at the other end. When it was safely down, they both flopped onto the leather cushions that they hadn't bothered to remove. The couch had been the last item in the truck, so Jen, their new third, was now officially moved in. Her laugh drifted down the hall from the master bedroom, where she and his father were putting together her bed.

"Another one down," Adam said. "How many to go?"

Jonas chuckled. Since moving to New Mexico, he'd given some thought to what he'd like to do with himself full time, but he hadn't progressed beyond ideas. He was too busy helping the new pack members get moved in and settled into their situations.

He'd helped his parents find a place and both had taken jobs at a local restaurant, to see what they thought of the food business. His dad had claimed that learning the business from the ground up was the only way to go. Jonas wasn't sure if they were really going to open up their own place, as he'd suggested, but they were having fun exploring the idea that they could do pretty much anything they wanted, so he figured he'd succeeded.

He'd helped Bill and Thomas, a couple in their forties who'd moved in from Florida, get settled into a trailer on a tract of land they'd decided to purchase. Thomas was a contractor and was going to build them a house when he had the time. Jonas had managed not to laugh out loud when Bill had rolled his eyes behind his husband's back.

Then there was Joe, who had come down from Pennsylvania to join them. He was a teacher, and the local high school had offered him a position to start immediately, so Jonas, his father, and Bill had done all the moving for their new second so he could get up to speed on his class without the stress of moving.

Olivia and Tasha Keogh, the mother and daughter who'd previously been in the Mesa Pack, were due to arrive the next day. There had been some discussion about the pair being a good fit for the pack, but everyone had agreed that the daughter wasn't thriving in Chicago, and Myra hoped they could turn the situation around with some TLC.

Cindy had told Jonas, privately, that she'd been concerned Adam might hold some resentment that Olivia hadn't made any move, in her old pack, to seek help regarding the rogue pack that had harmed Adam. But once Adam had met her at the party, even though he hadn't particularly liked her, he'd felt protective. So the invitation to join had been issued.

"Don't pretend you aren't loving building a pack from the ground up. I don't believe your grumpy persona for a second," Jonas said.

"Hmph. I'll have you know I was a bona fide hermit not that long ago."

"Yeah, but then you fell in love. That changes everything."

"Well. You're not wrong."

Adam rose, and Jonas heard the recently plugged-in refrigerator open and close before a water bottle appeared in front of his face. He grabbed the bottle and opened it while Adam came back around to join him on the couch.

When he'd taken a long drink, Jonas eyed Adam. "Cindy said you got stuck handling most of the details of getting the Keoghs set up?"

Adam sighed. "I suspect that woman's going to be a pain in our asses. Cindy was nice enough to give Myra some info from her landlady, and somehow that turned into me negotiating the lease and arrangements. Olivia is not shy about stating what she thinks, or what she wants."

"Tomorrow should be loads of fun, then."

"She's not terrible. Just...not particularly socially adept, I guess you could say."

"Which is saying something, coming from a recently reformed

hermit," Jonas said with a laugh. Adam lifted his bottle to him in salute.

Jen and Robert came down the hallway then, laughing. Jen put her toolbox down and looked around the room. "This is great guys, I really appreciate your help."

Jonas checked his watch. "Kickoff's in twenty minutes. You've got your bed set up, your fridge turned on and your TV plugged in. Abandon the boxes for tomorrow and come watch the game at my house."

"Son, I realize you've only been mated a few weeks, but don't you know better than to invite a bunch of people over for a game with no notice?"

Jonas smiled. "Trust me, Dad."

"I'm in," Adam said, pulling out his phone. "Let me see if Myra finished her work yet. She had a rush assignment she promised to get done today, even though it's Sunday. Otherwise she would have been here," he added to Jen.

"You going to call Mom?" Jonas asked his dad.

"I'll text her that we're going to watch the game, but she's working on a quilt and watching some girlie movies, she'll be glad to have another couple of hours without me underfoot."

They moved some boxes around to make sure Jen had clear paths to everything, and then headed out. He sent a little pulse down his mate link, smiling at the answering burst of joy at the knowledge that he was coming home.

Cindy had felt bad about not being able to help with the move, but she was hard at work on a couple of projects for the blog, and he'd told her Jen would understand. Just because she worked from home didn't mean she could be available in the middle of the day for someone else's needs.

When he'd said as much, he'd worried she would burst into tears and his heart had stopped, for just a second. Then he'd felt the love and appreciation coming from her, and he'd known the almost-tears were happy ones, not sad. Apparently people had not always understood that little fact.

He parked his car and by the time he was halfway up the walk, Cindy had the door open, bottle of beer in hand. He noted the wedge of lime sticking out from the top and smiled. His girl always knew the perfect drink to offer him, be it water, lemonade, a scotch, a beer or whatever. Sometimes it was something he'd never even heard of, but once he tasted it, it was exactly right.

She held the bottle out but he ignored it, wrapped his arms around her waist and lifted her up into the air. Which put her chest right in front of his face, so while that hadn't been his intent, he went ahead and nuzzled her, giving a little lick before he set her down. She opened her mouth, but he didn't give her a chance to say anything before claiming it for a kiss.

Her arms had gone around his shoulders when he lifted her, and now the beer thunked against his head, but he didn't care. He'd missed her. He'd only been gone for five hours, but he'd missed her.

When he finally pulled back—mostly because he heard the other cars pulling up, not because he wanted to stop—she had a look of such sweet pleasure that for a second, he was sorry he'd invited anyone over.

She looked past him. "Robert, I'm so glad you're here. Are you guys going to stay to watch the game with us?"

"If we're not intruding. We can go to the bar and grab some burgers there, if you're busy here."

"Don't be silly, come on in. Is Jen coming?" she asked, as Adam walked up and claimed a hug from her.

"She's right behind us," Jonas assured her as he gestured everyone into the house.

His dad headed towards the living room, then came to a stop.

Jonas had to laugh. It had been a normal living room when he'd left early that morning. Cindy had said she was going to work on some Super Bowl party recipe and decoration ideas for her blog, and he should encourage the others to come back to watch the game, so the food she made didn't go to waste. Now the living room looked like football come to life.

There was green felt covering the coffee table, with yardage lines in white. A console that was usually behind the couch had been moved up against a wall and draped in burlap. Above it was a banner of footballs. The console was covered in food. There was a watermelon that had been carved in the shape of a helmet, with fruit salad pouring out of it. There were rice crispy treats shaped like footballs, sliders, cups of dip with veggies sticking out of them, and so much more.

He shook his head and shoved his dad inside so he could pull his mate to him and give her another kiss. "You're something else. I can't wait to see how your pictures turned out."

"Pretty awesome, if I do say so myself."

"I've no doubt."

"Robert, Adam, there are beers and water bottles there in the bucket, but if you'd like something else, just let me know. There are sodas in the kitchen."

"This is great, Cindy, thanks. Myra says she'll be over in about an hour."

"Perfect, I'll save the parmesan-thyme-browned-butter popcorn for when she gets here, so it's nice and hot."

Adam groaned, putting a hand to his heart. "It's a good thing I love her. And that you have a table full of equally delicious-looking food over here. But just so you know, for future reference, I'm a popcorn kind of guy."

She laughed and kissed his cheek. "So noted. And how well you're matched, because it's one of Myra's favorites."

Adam looked pleased as he wandered over to the food table.

Jonas let Jen inside and made sure she was happy with the beer and water before he grabbed Cindy's hand and led her to their bedroom.

"Jonas, we are not getting it on while we have a house full of people," she said with a laugh as he backed her onto the bed. "Especially a room full of werewolves with excellent hearing."

He lay down and pulled her on top of him. "I know. But I missed you and want a little cuddle." He ran his hand up and down her back. "Did you get everything you needed? Are you done for the day?"

She melted into him. "I did, yes. Did Jen get settled in?"

"She still has a bunch to unpack, but she got most of the kitchen unboxed, and the bathroom. She and Dad set up her bed. She has her interview with the Sheriff's Department tomorrow."

She'd begun to draw shapes on his chest as they talked. He identified a heart, a spiral and a diamond. "Are you worried about figuring out your own work situation? I don't want you to feel like you have to help everyone get settled, to the detriment of yourself."

"Nah, I like it. It's nice to get a chance to spend some time with everyone early on while we're all getting used to being here, being together. I don't need to do anything, really, I just like to keep active. So as long as this is keeping me busy, and entertained, it's all good."

He heard a shout from the living room and sighed. "I guess we should go out there."

"You're the one who invited everyone," she reminded him.

"I didn't think I was up to the challenge of eating all your practice food myself." He pinched her butt lightly. "And you totally knew I would, there's no way that whole spread was just practice. I was happy to invite them, until I had you in my arms."

"Sweet talker." She kissed him hard and fast and rolled away.

CHAPTER SIX

C indy shooed Jen and Robert out after the game, assuring Robert he needed to get home to his wife, and telling Jen she had plenty to do at her own place, and didn't need to get stuck with cleanup here.

Joe, who had shown up at halftime, handed Jen the bag of leftovers he'd put together for her, setting his own bag on the table by the door. Cindy liked their new second. He was young, but strong. He'd been third at his previous pack, and she'd been curious to see where he'd land, since their pack had only Jen in the hierarchy when he'd arrived. Myra told her they'd all—Myra, Adam, Jen and Joe— had dinner together, and by the end of it, had no trouble setting the ranks.

"Food's all sorted," he told her. "Do you want me to pull down the decorations?"

"That would be great, thanks." She folded up the burlap she'd used on the console. "How are you finding things at the high school?"

"It's so different, but I'm enjoying that. I think the whole school is smaller than the freshman class at my last school. So there are different challenges, but definitely some fun opportunities, as well."

"And then there's the weather," she said.

He laughed. "Yeah, I'm trying to get used to that. It's bizarre, I was talking to my mom last night and had to seriously resist teasing her about the differences in our weather."

"Are your parents going to come out and visit?"

"Probably in the summer. Hey, I hear we're having another meet-the-potential-pack party soon. Do we have that many more people interested in joining?"

"There's only going to be about ten this time."

"I'm hoping there will be someone we like as first or fourth. I don't like having only four of us for a hierarchy."

She had gathered all the decorations into a tub and now he snapped the lid on it. "There, that wasn't so bad." She rubbed the small of her back. She'd been on her feet most of the day. "Even with the small number of us, you feel a gap?" she asked as Jonas, Myra and Adam joined them from the kitchen. Jonas tugged her hand until she fell onto the sofa beside him.

"It's not bad," Myra answered for him. "But I'll feel better when we have at least one more. Whether that's a new first or fourth, or even a mate for our lovely second or third, doesn't matter." She sat in Adam's lap, on the cozy club chair that Jonas had added to the living room when he'd moved in.

"Speaking of potential new people coming to the party," Myra continued with a serious look that caught Cindy's attention. "Someone you know called to feel me out about coming for an exploratory visit." She paused a beat. "Brenda."

She must have stiffened, because Jonas hands started to rub up and down her arms. She leaned back into him, relaxing. "I'm surprised. I thought she was pretty happy in Texas. Mom's never mentioned anything about her looking to move elsewhere."

"Who is this person?" Adam asked.

"Lots of wolves who've never really thought about moving started thinking about it when we began this," Myra reminded her. She turned to look at her mate, over her shoulder. "Brenda is fourth in the pack Cindy grew up in"

"I just realized how strange it is that she never moved up in all these years," Cindy mused.

"You don't like her," Adam said.

Cindy squirmed. That wasn't something she would have stated out loud. "I don't dislike her, exactly. I've hardly even thought about her in years. I just didn't particularly like her, and I didn't really respect her."

"Ouch," Joe said. "Not a good thing for a young pack member to feel about their fourth."

"We don't need her," Adam said.

Cindy sighed. "There's no reason not to have her come for a visit. Maybe she's changed. I certainly have. She might click. We do need a fourth, as you were just saying." She gestured between Joe and Myra.

Adam snorted. "Why waste anyone's time? I trust your instincts, and if your instincts said she wasn't great, then that's enough for me."

That warmed her considerably, but still, she didn't want to be unfair to someone who had never hurt her. "What did she say when she called?" Cindy asked Myra.

"That she's been watching the thread on the forum and is excited to see that we're settling in. She said she contacted an old friend who lives out this way and owns that big truck stop by the highway. About twenty minutes from here?" She waited while they all nodded that they knew the place. "She said she found out he needs a new manager, and she told him she might have someone who would work. Asked me if we had any new pack members needing a job that she could recommend."

"That's nice," Cindy said.

Jonas harrumphed. "Sounds to me like she knows she needs to bring something to the table besides her mere presence."

Cindy frowned. "I don't know if that's fair. She probably didn't even mention me." She looked questioningly at Myra.

"Well, she said she wanted to check in and see if I thought it would be okay to visit. She didn't want to make anyone feel uncomfortable."

"Anyone," Cindy repeated flatly.

"Yeah, it was pretty clear she meant you, and knows that we're best friends."

"Look, she never did anything for me to complain about. I worked in her office for a while, and I didn't think she made the best decisions. But I was new, didn't even work there a year. So maybe I just didn't know enough to understand why she was making the choices she was making."

"What kinds of choices?" Adam asked.

"She was an insurance broker, and it seemed to me that she was steering her clients towards products that were more about making her the most money than giving them the best of what they needed. Not that what she gave them was bad," she added quickly. "Just maybe not the best options for their situations. But, again, she knew her business much better than I did. It just squicked me out, so I decided to look for a new job, and that's when I realized that I didn't have to stay close to home. I could explore any new city, any new job, that I wanted to."

Myra frowned. "I assume at least some of her clients were pack members?"

"Yes. I'm still not sure if that made it worse or not. I mean, it's sucky no matter who the clients are. But she's hierarchy, so…"

"Seriously, I don't see any reason to bother with her coming out here," Adam reiterated.

Cindy was frustrated. While she really appreciated the thought, she absolutely did not want to be responsible for the alpha couple summarily rejecting Brenda's request to join. Not based solely on the opinion of someone she hadn't even seen in decades.

"Because if you don't, she'll be able to say to anyone who wants to listen that she wasn't allowed because Cindy doesn't like her. And Cindy isn't going to go around telling people why that's so, which means you're putting her in an awkward position," Jonas said.

Myra nodded. "That's true. If she comes out, we can tell her that we never asked Cindy's opinion on whether she should be allowed to join the pack."

"Okay. But seriously, try to keep an open mind. Give her an actual chance," Cindy said. "And we should find out if Olivia would be interested in the job Brenda mentioned."

Everyone turned to look at Adam, who sighed. "I'll tell her about it tomorrow, when I help her move in."

"Thanks." Myra gave him a kiss on the cheek. "Cindy, do you want to do a theme for the next party, or should we go plain?"

Cindy gave a huge gasp. "Did you really just ask me that?"

Myra laughed. "Well, you're still newly mated, and you have your own business, and maybe you're busy."

"Uh, yeah, I have my own business, where I need to show theme parties. Don't worry, I'll handle it. And still find time for my mate."

Jonas wrapped his arms around her middle. "You better, or I'll be forced to help you with the party decorations, and I don't know if that would actually be helpful or harmful."

"Good plan," Joe said. "Screw it up badly enough now, and she'll never ask you for help again."

"Says the guy without a mate or a girlfriend," Cindy said, laughing.

"Hey! I just moved here, like, a minute ago. Give a guy a chance." He glanced at his watch. "Anyone up for a quick run?"

"Sounds like a plan," Adam said, standing with a laughing Myra still in his arms. He let her slide down his body until her feet found the floor.

Cindy glanced behind her at Jonas, who gave her a look that basically said sure, why not? She rose from the couch.

"We're in. Jonas, if you'll put this bin in my office, I'll lock the front door."

They used the back door and walked about half a mile, chatting quietly as they exited the neighborhood, but keeping alert for any signs of other neighbors out for a nighttime stroll. Cindy had found a nice spot that was out of the way and provided some cover for making their change and storing their clothing. Normally, she and

Jonas would change at home and just leave by the back door, but there were too many of them to chance stealthily running through the neighborhood in wolf form.

With Myra and Adam there, Cindy and Jonas didn't need to worry about having the strength to change back to human after such a short run. The alpha pair would be able to lend them the strength to get it done. Joe was strong enough to make the change back himself.

They separated out a little bit, then changed. Cindy brushed against Jonas as soon as they were both fully wolf. She loved him, no matter what form she was in, but there was something so simple and perfect about being with her mate in wolf form.

He licked her muzzle then turned to pick up the clothes they'd bundled together and bring it to the large rock they'd use to hide their belongings. Myra followed with their shoes, and added them to the pile the others had put together.

Seeing that everyone was set, Adam gave off a howl and sped away. Snorting, Myra gave chase, with Jonas and Cindy hot on her heels. Joe took the rear, and Cindy knew he was going slower than he needed to in order to cover their backs, even though they didn't have any reason to be concerned about the area. Their new second liked to be cautious, she'd learned. Something she appreciated in her hierarchy.

When they were well away from town, Adam circled around and bounced in front of Jonas, inviting him to play. They whirled and chased, bowed and nipped, making slow progress forward but having a lot of fun. Cindy huffed, her wolf version of a snicker, when Myra bounded between them then took off like a shot, inviting a game of chase. The men answered immediately, taking off after her.

Cindy wasn't interested in top speed tonight. She loped along, Joe keeping pace with her. She wished the cloud cover would go away and they could see the beautiful stars, and have better moonlight, but she tasted rain in the air and figured they'd be getting some by the next evening.

She stepped on a sharp rock and whined a little, slowing to a stop so she could shake it free from her paw. The burst of concern came down her mate bond immediately, but she let Jonas know she was fine. The sharp sting had faded as soon as it had hit. Joe waited while she tested her next step to be sure the rock had shaken loose, then gave her face a quick lick and they continued on.

They ran and played for an hour before resting in a big pile, listening to the sounds of the desert and enjoying just being together as a pack. After a while, Myra stood, and they all followed, ready to head back to home and bed.

JONAS CLIMBED down from the ladder and surveyed his handiwork. Olivia was in the kitchen unpacking boxes and Tasha was in her bedroom, making the bed. He'd just finished adding brackets to the large bookcase that had found a home in the living room, attaching it firmly to the wall.

He and Bill had carted everything in from the truck by late morning. The Keoghs didn't have a lot of material possessions. Except books. They had quite a few boxes of books, which he had no complaints about. Bill had set up the television while Jonas helped Olivia hang curtains. Then Bill had left and Jonas had taken care of the bookcase. Unlike Jen, neither Olivia nor Tasha had bed frames that needed to be put together. There really wasn't much more to do, other than actually empty all the boxes he'd dragged in.

He didn't think they'd love him opening up their boxes, and he was getting pretty hungry, so he went to the kitchen.

"Olivia, how about I go pick up lunch for all of us and bring it back here. In the meantime, take a look around and let me know if there's anything else you could use my help with before I head out."

The doorbell rang before she had a chance to respond. She looked questioningly at him, but he just shrugged. Until he thought about it, tuned into his bond, and realized it was his mate on the other side of the door. And chances were pretty much guaranteed that she had food.

Olivia had opened the door by the time he'd made his realization and headed over to join her. He took the Crock-Pot out of Cindy's hands, accepting a kiss, all while she spoke to Olivia.

"I figured you guys would be hungry about now, and not in the mood to go find any food. "That's a pot of chili." She held up a grocery bag. "This is paper plates and plastic utensils, in case you haven't unpacked dishes yet, and sour cream, avocado, cheese and jalapenos, for toppings."

Olivia blinked at her for a minute, clearly shocked. Then she nodded. "That's very kind of you, Cindy. Thank you. Jonas was just suggesting food, so your timing is perfect. Jonas, if you let Tasha know, I'll get things set up on the table."

"I have another bag in the car with drinks. I'll go grab it." Cindy didn't wait for a response.

Jonas saw that Olivia didn't move, just stood staring at the still open door.

"Is she overwhelming?" he asked softly.

"No." Olivia shook her head—and turned to Jonas with a smile. The first real smile he'd seen from her. "No. She's extremely kind, and so are you. This was very thoughtful of her. I was going to buy you lunch, as a tiny thank you for all your help today."

"No need, I'm happy to do my part in getting you and Tasha settled here. Everyone in the pack is starting over, and we all need each other to make that transition as easy as possible."

Cindy came back through the door, and Olivia gave him one last smile before heading to the little dining area next to the kitchen. The apartment wasn't grand, but it was set up nicely, had two bedrooms, and was close to the high school Tasha would be attending.

He went down the short hall and stuck his head through Tasha's door. She'd made her bed and was hanging clothes in the closet.

"Hey, Cindy brought lunch for everyone. Ready to take a break?"

She smiled at him, not quite meeting his gaze. Her shyness made him nervous about her ability to find friends at the new school. He'd have to ask Myra and Adam if any of the new potential pack members had teenagers. He imagined it would be a lot easier for Tasha to get close to another wolf, so she wouldn't have to hide such an important part of herself.

He stepped back and let her proceed him down the hall, where the delicious smell of chili made his stomach growl.

CINDY WOULDN'T EXACTLY CALL the conversation around lunch lively, but she managed to get a couple of smiles and comments from both Olivia and Tasha. And the general air of negativity she'd sensed during her first meeting with Olivia seemed to have faded away. She was glad she'd had the idea to come with lunch.

She looked around the apartment. "Nice place. I like the park across the street."

"We'll see," Olivia said. "Some parks turn into drug dens and homeless camps at night."

Cindy bit back a smile. "I think Jonas mentioned the crime rates in this neighborhood are pretty low, but it's definitely a good idea to keep an eye out and see what it's really like."

"You'll let me know if there's anything questionable," Jonas added.

Olivia nodded. Tasha played with her food.

"Olivia, if it would help, Tasha and I could go to the store to get your groceries while you get some more boxes unpacked."

"I can pay for our groceries."

"Mom!"

Cindy wasn't sure how to respond, but Jonas leaned in and looked into Olivia's eyes. "She wasn't thinking about money one way or the other. Just about helping you get settled. It wasn't very long ago that she moved, and she remembers what a pain in the butt it is."

Olivia watched him for a second, then turned to Cindy. Whatever she saw on Cindy's face seemed to reassure her. "All right, then. I'm sorry. That would be very helpful, I can give Tasha my card."

"That's perfect then. We'll just get the basics, unless you want to take a minute to do up a list?"

"No, thank you. Tasha will know the basics, and we can do a big shop tomorrow."

"Excellent. You need anything while I'm there, Jonas?"

"No, baby, I'm good."

When they climbed into her car, Cindy slanted a look at the quiet teenager. "Have you had a chance to explore the local radio stations?"

Tasha shook her head.

"Want to give it a go?" Cindy gestured towards the radio.

She headed towards the store as the radio jumped from commercial to music to talking and back again. It was a short drive to the market, but by the time they pulled into the parking lot, Taylor Swift was signing and Tasha had sat back in her seat with a smile to Cindy.

"Good choice." She pulled into a parking space and cranked up the volume. Then she met Tasha's gaze and started singing along. Loudly. It took a few seconds, but then the girl joined in, a wide grin on her face as they sang the chorus with considerable lack of skill.

When the song ended, Cindy turned the car off and laughed. "We suck, but in a totally awesome way."

"Yeah."

It was said softly, but Cindy visualized high-fiving herself while playing it cool on the outside. Tasha grabbed a cart and they headed inside.

An hour later, Cindy was feeling pretty good as she returned to her house. Mission accomplished. She'd gotten to feed and kiss her man, make Olivia feel welcomed, and she'd actually had a conversation with Tasha where the teenager had participated fully.

Now she could finish up the plans for the weekend party at the pack house while Jonas was off helping his mom plant her herb garden. Apparently it was a tradition they'd had when he'd lived in

New York, that they hadn't been able to enjoy together since he'd moved away. They'd invited her to join them, but she'd thought they could use the time together. Besides, she had a black thumb.

She got to work printing out some colorful printables that were supposed to make party decorating easy for anyone. Cindy was ready to post them on the blog, if they worked as advertised. Which she thought they probably would. She had a nice stack of them going, but had to keep a close eye on them to make sure the paper was lined up correctly, so when her phone rang with her mom's ringtone. She bit back a sigh.

JONAS WASN'T WORRIED, exactly, as he walked into the house several hours later. He just had a niggling of concern. Cindy always met him at the door if she was home when he arrived, usually with a drink, always with a kiss. He knew she was home. He could feel her nearness along that amazing link they shared.

He dumped the grocery bag he was carrying on the side table and headed for her office. She was sitting with her chin cupped in her hand, staring at her computer monitor. He came all the way up to her and kissed the top of her head. She blinked at him for a second, then nearly bonked his chin as she jumped to her feet.

"Oh, wow, sorry. I was a million miles away."

"No need to be sorry for that. You okay? Is it the party?"

"No, that's pretty much squared away." She wrapped her arms around his waist and went up on her tiptoes to give him a proper kiss. He hummed his pleasure and pulled her in tighter for a minute, before letting her loose and pulling back a bit so he could see her face.

"The blog?"

"No, that's just the normal amount of annoying that work always is, except for when it's not."

He smiled at that, understanding the joys of working a job you love. "What would help? Can you put me to work on something? Or

I can take you out to dinner? I stopped at the store and got steaks and potatoes. We can have them tonight, or freeze the steaks for later. It's no Snickers bar, but they'd probably go a ways towards making you feel better."

"Steak and potatoes sound perfect. I'll even volunteer to man the microwave for the potatoes."

"Oh no, this is my deal. If you're done with work, you can hang out and keep me company, though. Or go take a hot bath and I'll bring you some wine."

She kissed his chin. "I'll come hang with you."

"Want me to grab one of your aprons?"

"Sure, you can borrow one if you'd like."

He rolled his eyes at her. For some reason, he loved her colorful aprons. Rather, he loved them when *she* was wearing them. At least he'd gotten her to smile.

He took her hand and led her to the bag he'd left in the living room, then on to the kitchen. The glass of wine came first, one for each of them. He kept quiet as he unloaded the groceries and pulled out the large cast iron skillet. It wasn't until he was cranking the pepper mill over the steaks that she spoke.

"My mom called a while ago."

Ah. She hadn't spoken of her family much. She'd called her parents, and her brother and his wife, when they'd first mated, but when he'd asked if she wanted to go out for a visit, she'd said she'd rather wait until the pack was a little more settled.

"What did she have to say?"

"That she knew Brenda was coming out here to see if she wanted to join our pack, and I better not be immature and sabotage her with the alphas. Or words to that affect, though it took her a good five minutes to say it all."

He just looked at her. "Seriously?"

She nodded. "Yep. I told her I was an adult and perfectly capable of acting like one, and Myra, Adam, Joe and Jen were all perfectly capable of deciding on their own who should join our pack."

Jonas couldn't hold back a snort. "Yeah, they're perfectly capable of siding with you, whether you ask them to or not. And it's none of her business if they do so."

"Well, I decided she didn't really need to know any of that."

"Probably a good call." He finished seasoning the meat and put both steaks in the large pan, then went to kneel in front of her chair. Her legs opened to invite him in closer. "I hate that you don't have a great relationship with your family. What the hell is wrong with them?"

"It's not a terrible relationship. It's just not great."

"Yeah, but you being you, the person that you are, that's terrible."

She blinked at him. "I guess I followed that." She sighed. "I just... they never really got me. They think my brother's the greatest thing ever. And he *is* pretty awesome, I love him. I was worried that they'd be awful to his mate when he found her, but they embraced her. They just find me vaguely disappointing."

"Again, you being you, I just don't understand that. I mean, do they not know you at all? The things you've accomplished with your business? The roll you've played in your pack?"

She raised her eyebrows at him.

"If you don't think Myra's bragged on you, you don't know your best friend very well."

"Heh. Well. It would almost be easier if they were awful, then I'd just walk away."

"That's why it was so easy for you to move to St. Louis."

"Yeah, I missed my brother, especially when he mated and started having kids, but I Skype with them and go visit once a year or so." She kissed him. "Go start the potatoes, I'm fine."

He gave her a playfully fierce look, then got up to do as she'd said. He needed to feed her. He poked holes in the potatoes and got them into the microwave, then flipped the steaks.

"Your brother is third in his pack?"

"Yes. I think you'll like him. I know we need to go out there so you can meet everyone. Or invite them out here. I kind of don't want my parents in my space, though, so I'd rather go out there."

"If that's what you want, that's what we'll do. How did you leave it with your mom?"

She blushed. "I told her I was about to start a meeting and had to go."

"There's nothing wrong with that."

"I should be strong enough to just tell her that I don't want to talk about Brenda and if she has nothing else to say, we're done."

He pulled her up and into his arms. "Baby. She's your mom, and as much as you tell yourself that you shouldn't care that she's not as impressed by you as she should be, which is the truth, it's not so easy to stop wanting her approval."

"You're pretty smart. And you have awesome parents. I already love them."

"They love you, too."

He left one arm around her and pulled her to the stove, opened the microwave and turned the potatoes. "You might feel better once we go visit. Instead of worrying about it."

"Possibly."

"Or we can just pretend they don't exist, you can block your mom's number on your phone, and we can hang out with people we like and respect, and who return the favor."

She gave him a wan smile. "I'm not quite there, but I'll keep that as a plan C."

The microwave beeped and he turned the stove off. "Let's eat. You'll feel better, for sure."

"I'm already better, just being with you. But steak definitely won't hurt."

CHAPTER SEVEN

Cindy pushed away from the table, absolutely full. The pack had gathered together for dinner, to celebrate the fact that both Jen and Olivia had gotten jobs. Jen had been hired at the Sheriff's Office and Olivia had been hired as the manager at the truck stop, after being recommended by Brenda.

"Tasha, your mom's Brussels sprouts were amazing, and I can't believe those words even just came out of my mouth."

Tasha, sitting next to her, laughed. "I know, right? Brussels sprouts and amazing don't seem like they should go together, but she has a way with them. Of course, the fact that there's bacon involved helps considerably."

Cindy cheered inwardly at Tasha's willingness to have an actual conversation. She risked pushing it further.

"How was your first day at school?"

Tasha looked thoughtful before she replied. "It made me feel better, knowing that Joe was there if I needed him, but I didn't. None of my teachers seem like crazy people, so far, and you can usually tell pretty quickly."

Cindy laughed. "That's good."

"I've never been to such a small school. I think most of the kids have known each other for years. On the one hand, that's not so great. But on the other hand, they're curious to get some new blood in there, I think."

Cocking her head, Cindy hazarded a guess. "Especially the guys?"

The blush was answer enough, but Tasha nodded. "Yeah, it's kind of weird, but kind of nice, but also I have to be careful. Girls can get stupid with jealousy."

Cindy had to smile at the adorable eye roll that came with the statement.

"You're not wrong, but I'm glad that there's some openness there. Now you just need to find a girl posse so you can get all the dirt on the guys."

Tasha's face went serious and grabbed Cindy's full attention.

"I just want to thank you guys for taking Mom and me in. I know Mom can be a little...difficult. She doesn't mean to be, she's just used to having to bitch and complain to get heard."

"You guys were in a very dysfunctional pack. I can't even imagine how difficult that must have been. If there's anything you can think of that I can do to help with both of you feeling like welcome and active parts of this pack, please let me know."

"She was really, really pleased that she was offered the opportunity to apply for that job. And that Adam made it clear it was something that had come up, but if she didn't feel it was right for her, that was all right, too." She hesitated, and Cindy gave her an encouraging nod.

"In Chicago, she had a hard time finding a good job. Some of the pack members would tell her things, like they saw a help-wanted sign at the fast food restaurant." She paused again, glanced down the table to find her mom talking to Myra and Bill. "It's not that she thinks she's above a job like that, but she's very smart, and very good at office work and managing, so..."

"It probably felt like people were demeaning her."

"Yeah. Not intentionally, but, yeah. She hated having to ask the pack for help, but everything is very expensive out there. Anyway, I'm so glad Myra and Adam were willing to let us come here."

Cindy put her arm around the girl's shoulders. "Me, too, honey. If your homework's not bad this weekend, and you're interested, I'd love some help setting up for the party on Saturday. And, just in case it hasn't been made clear already, Adam and Myra are going to want your opinion on the people who ask to join. So make sure you try and talk to people, get a good sense of them."

Tasha blinked at her. "My opinion? Are...are you sure?" She looked doubtful.

"One hundred percent sure. They'll have to decide, of course, but they'll want to hear any strong feelings you have, one way or the other.

"Okay. I know Mom is looking forward to meeting Brenda, and thanking her for the opportunity."

"She'll be glad it turned out to be a good fit."

"I'm going to grab dessert. Looks like Joe made a cake. Do you want a piece?"

Cindy laughed and rubbed her stomach. "Not yet, honey, I'm still full. Thanks."

She made a mental note to let Myra know that the Keoghs seemed to be settling in just fine. A quick look around the room found her mate chatting with Myra. She started in their direction, only to be hailed by Bill and Thomas.

"Cindy, we need you to settle a debate," Thomas said.

"Oh dear. This isn't going to go well for me, is it?"

Bill's lips twitched, but he pulled on a serious face. "You're a life-style blogger, right?"

"Riiiight?"

"So you have your thumb on the pulse of what's going on out there. Right?"

"Uh-huh, sure, let's go with that."

"Tiny homes. Are they the future? The smart, responsible way to live in the new millennium?"

"Tiny homes. Okay, well, I guess my question would be, even if nine out of ten people said tiny homes were the best thing ever, does that really have anything to do with where you personally want to live?"

"Ha!" Bill said, smacking Thomas on the arm with the back of his hand.

"But then again, sometimes you need to hear about a thing several times before you start to incorporate it into your thinking, and allow for it as a possibility. When something sort of radical comes along, it can be hard to take it seriously until you've heard it enough that you just can't ignore it."

"Ha yourself," Thomas said, smirking.

"So, I can't say I've done any research on tiny homes myself, but certainly the idea of being minimalist and being conscious of environmental impact is good. But then, sometimes space is good as well. I guess my question would be, aren't you living in a trailer right now? Isn't that pretty much the same thing?" She smiled at Jonas as he joined them, wrapping his arms around her and leaning his chin on her head.

"The trailer is okay, but it hasn't been optimized for long-term living, like I would want." Thomas was frowning as he considered.

"We've done pretty well so far. We had a fairly large home before, so we still have a lot of stuff in storage," Bill said. "I'm already starting to forget what half of it is."

Thomas nudged him. "See, we don't need all that stuff."

"Yeah, except I've already had to stop you three times from ordering things online because we have them in storage, but you were looking for them."

"That's true. We do need our things. But I bet we can get rid of a lot of it."

"Probably, but we don't have room for any of it right now."

"Because we're not optimized!"

"Well, then, maybe we should do that and see if we can bring our stuff out of storage. Then we'll know if we can do something like that long term." Bill leaned over and kissed Thomas' cheek.

Thomas smiled. "Good plan."

They both looked at Cindy. "Thanks for your help."

She laughed. "I don't think I did much, but you're very welcome."

They wandered off and Cindy turned around within the circle of Jonas' arms.

"Hey, handsome."

"Hey, beautiful. You about ready to go home?"

"I still need a piece of cake. I was too full of dinner to eat it right away."

"It's damn good cake, you don't want to miss out. Want me to get you a piece?"

"Let's get some to go and head home."

When they were in the car, she gave him a rundown of her conversation with Tasha. "You know how I like to think about life in layers?"

"Like with your blog."

"Exactly. I'm constantly going back to older posts and trying to see how I can take whatever the post was about—be it baking a great cake, organizing your house, diving into finances, whatever—and go to the next level on that one thing. Sometimes there's nothing else to add, but a lot of times I find that we can go down another layer. Get deeper into it."

"I get it. I'm enjoying going deeper with you."

She slanted him a look and he laughed.

"No. Well, yes, I very much enjoy pushing deep into you, but that's not what I mean. I feel like every other day, I see more of you, and I'm constantly amazed at how beautiful you are, down to your soul."

The fact that he got it, got her, was still something she marveled over. "I'm enjoying peeling your layers, too."

"But that wasn't your point, I think you were going to tell me something else."

She blinked. "Oh, yeah, right. Olivia. I was going to say that I think living with that bad pack, she had to give herself an outer shell. A hard layer to protect herself behind. I mean, I don't really know all the details, but it had to have been very unhealthy. And she had a child to raise, on her own."

"Myra didn't give you all the details?"

"No, not really any more than was made public."

"I asked Olivia about Tasha's father. He was a soldier, killed in Iraq years ago. He was from Mesa, and they moved there when they mated."

Cindy shook her head, sadness seeping through her enough that Jonas reached out and took her hand. "I assumed she was from Mesa. I wonder why didn't she turn to her home pack, contact her family or her old alpha about what was happening with the rogue pack. I mean, I still don't get why none of the Mesa pack contacted National, but you'd think she had people she trusted from her home pack, right?" She slapped her hand on her knee. "No. I can't second guess her decisions when I don't have the facts. I just have to believe that she thought the only way to protect herself and her child was to stay silent." She drew in a deep breath. "But now they're here, and my point is that I have to remember not to judge her by that hard exterior layer. I need to look deeper. I was really glad when she jumped at the chance to interview for the job Brenda found. And tonight it seemed like she was more open to getting to know people, not so on the defensive."

"I think, when we met her at first, she was convinced she wouldn't be allowed to join and preparing herself for that disappointment." He let go of her hand as he pulled the car into their driveway.

"I think you're right. Anyway, I'm glad things are on the right track now, I'm really happy that our little pack is coming together and supporting each other."

They went into the house and she went straight to the refrigerator to get milk for their cake. "Do you want your piece now?"

"Yes, please. Are you worried about Brenda coming this weekend?"

She poured them both glasses and met him at the table. "Nope.

Either she'll have changed, and I won't mind her joining, or she won't have, and she won't be invited to join."

"What if she has a good outer layer and a rotten core?"

"I think it would take a much smarter person than Brenda to fool Adam, Myra, Joe and Jen."

He raised his milk glass to her in a toast as she took her first bite of cake. "Oh, man, this really *is* good."

JONAS ENJOYED the second piece of cake, but more, he enjoyed watching Cindy devour hers with a singular focus. He had a feeling Joe would be getting interrogated about recipes next time Cindy was in a room with him.

Damn, he loved the woman. She was beautiful, kind, and generous, almost to a fault. It made him crazy that her parents didn't see that in her. Her observations about Olivia were a perfect example. He had to admit, he'd been annoyed with Olivia for being snippy when he'd first met her, and for her maneuvering him into helping her with the move. If she had straight up just asked him, he wouldn't have thought twice about helping. But now he realized she'd probably been afraid of being rejected for such a simple request, and had gotten used to having to do things the more difficult way. Which just turned people off her, and that became a vicious cycle.

But his Cindy had seen through the negativity, and now he thought he'd be seeing Olivia with different eyes. And remembering to take a closer look at others who might deserve that second chance.

Which, unfortunately, probably meant she was right to insist that everyone give Brenda a chance, even though he kind of just wanted to hate her on principle.

He forked up his last bite of cake and polished off his milk. His mate was watching him, having finished her piece already, her eyes sparkling.

"What's going on inside that head of yours?" he asked.

"Well, I was thinking about cake and milk and things that go really well together, and then I was looking at you and thinking that *you* would go really well with whiskey. I don't know why, just that smoky, smooth bite of a good whiskey seemed like it would really compliment your skin, and so I was trying to thinking of what kind of whiskey we have in the pantry and if it was good enough for you."

He blinked at her, his brain having gone numb at some point during her response. Then, without a conscious decision to get up, he stood fast enough to knock his chair over and kissed her, pressing her hard into the back of her chair.

She hummed her appreciation as he tasted the cake and milk and all that was his Cindy. He wrapped his arms around her and stood, her legs automatically going around his hips. When he pressed her up against the wall, she pulled her lips free of his.

"Does this mean you're not going to let me pour whiskey on you and drink my fill?"

"Later." He tried to work the button on her jeans open. "Maybe you should start wearing skirts."

She laughed and pulled her legs down. He dropped to his knees and had her pants open and pulled down to her thighs in seconds, her underwear only a second after. He teased her with licks and nibbles, up and down and all around, until she was moaning, her legs, trapped by her jeans, trembling beneath his hands.

He froze when the scent that had been teasing him for a few minutes actually registered with his brain. He looked up, found her watching him with a soft look. She nodded.

She was ovulating. It didn't mean she would get pregnant if they had sex. But she could.

He kissed her belly on either side, where he vaguely imagined her ovaries were.

"I have some condoms. Somewhere." He cleared his suddenly tight throat.

She smiled at him and shook her head, slowly. He felt her desire through their bond, a perfect match for his.

He resumed his path south.

"Jonas, let me—"

He sucked her clit between his lips, enjoying her shocked cry of release that followed almost immediately. Slightly sated, he helped her down to the floor and pulled her pants off. She reached down and worked on her socks while he pulled his shirt over his head with a laugh.

"It's kind of chilly, baby, maybe you should leave your socks on."

She stuck her tongue out at him and pulled her own shirt off. "You know, there are rooms in this house that are carpeted. There's a bed. Two, actually. There's a couch. We should probably find one of those things."

"We can do that." He kind of grunted out the last word as she launched herself at him, landing him on his back, her knees bracketing his hips, her hands pressing firmly down on his shoulders, her lips hovering an inch above his.

"Or we can stay here." He brought his hands up her sides, then curved them over her breasts.

She kissed him, softly at first, then harder as he squeezed her breasts, toyed with her nipples. She moved her hips until she was sitting on his hard length, her wet heat an invitation he wanted to accept, but he couldn't quite bear to stop her just yet.

He abandoned her breasts and moved to cup her butt. His fingers digging into the luscious globes, he rocked her against him. She cried out, pulling her mouth away from his. He took advantage, rolling them so he was on top, her legs automatically encircling him as he slid into her.

"Oh yeah," she moaned. "More, Jonas."

Her demand, her need of him, was everything. He slid his hands under her head so she wasn't grinding it against the hard floor, his fingers tangling in her silky hair. He kissed her throat as he slid back out, nipped as he thrust in again. He kept the rhythm for several minutes, refusing to increase his pace no matter how much the heels digging into his ass encouraged otherwise.

When he stopped kissing her, she opened her eyes, met his gaze.

"So deep," he murmured.

She smiled. "I feel you in my soul."

Her hands came up to cup his face, and he had to stop moving.

"I see you, too. So beautiful. Everything I needed and didn't even know."

Her words filled him. He'd always been a people person, been good with relationships with friends and family. But he'd never known how pale that was to holding his everything in his arms, and knowing he was that, to her, as well. He wanted nothing more than to fill that position for her for the rest of his life.

She smiled, then arched her hips. "So deep," she said with a grin.

He began to move again, slow and steady, their gazes locked. Her breath had evened out, but now it hitched again. She pulled her bottom lip between her teeth, and he wanted to do the same, but not when it meant losing eye contact. He ground his hips, knowing he hit her clit by the way her eyes went vague. Okay, soul searching satisfied for now, he let go.

She moaned as he sped up and pulled his face down to hers. Giving her what she wanted, what she demanded, he kissed her hard and fierce, his mind going blank as he found his release. He had just enough awareness to listen as her moans turned to a cry of release, her body shuddering under his.

He collapsed to the side, pulling her with him so that she lay mostly across his chest instead of on the floor.

CHAPTER EIGHT

S etting up the party took hardly any time, since Cindy had both Tasha and Jonas helping out. And she had her lists. The other two fought over who would get to climb the ladder to hang the banners and lights, but in the end, they both shared the job. She rolled her eyes at their antics, but loved seeing how quickly Tasha seemed to be opening up and losing some of her shyness.

Myra had asked everyone in the pack to come about half an hour before the guests were to arrive, so they gathered in the library. Cindy sat in Jonas' lap and looked to her alphas.

"I know we just had our pack meeting last week, so we don't need to go over everything again, I just wanted to take a minute to say I'm really happy with how this pack has pulled together so far. Everyone taking time to help each other get settled in has been awesome. We've got a great group going, but we need more people. Try and talk to everyone who comes today and let someone in the hierarchy know your thoughts on them."

She paused to take a sip of her wine. "It's probably impossible that we'll have one hundred percent agreement from everyone in the pack on all the potential new members, so please don't be hurt if someone you like gets rejected or someone you don't like gets accepted. We value your opinions and impressions and need to gather all of them to make an informed decision."

Adam put his arm around her shoulder. "And remember that while first impressions are critical, and instincts are a part of who we are, there are people who can surprise you, so don't make the mistake of locking in your opinions on someone too strongly. Everyone knows I was a cantankerous hermit when Myra met me, and look at us now."

"Now that you're a cantankerous busybody?" Cindy asked demurely.

Everyone laughed, and they all chatted easily until Adam looked up. "We have visitors, people. Let's do this thing."

They followed him to the door and greeted their first guests, the Chang family from Toronto, who wanted to escape the weather. Parents, teenage girl and middle-school boy. Cindy put her arm around Tasha and nudged her towards the girl.

"Hi, Blaire, I'm Cindy, and this is Tasha. Tasha just started at the school you would be going to, last week. She said so far it's pretty okay. Have you been to the States before, or is this your first time?"

By the time she'd maneuvered the girls to the snack table, they were deep in conversation. Cindy glanced to the parents and met Sofia Chang's gaze. The woman gave her a happy smile and a nod. Pleased, Cindy moved to Jonas, who was talking to an older woman who'd just arrived.

"Latisha Bogan, meet my mate, Cindy. Cindy, Mrs. Bogan is visiting from Peachwood Pack, near Atlanta."

Cindy was gentle taking the elderly woman's hand into her own, but had to smile when the woman's strong grip surprised her. "It's a pleasure to meet you, Mrs. Bogan."

"I've already told Jonas to call me Latisha, and you will to. The young ones can call me Miss Latisha. I was a kindergarten teacher for thirty years, so that's what I'm used to."

"What brings you to New Mexico?" Cindy asked.

"My George passed on a couple of years ago. He wasn't the healthiest wolf around, and wouldn't listen to a word I said about diet and exercise. Overweight wolves are the exception, I know, but that was George."

Jonas' fingers twined with hers and she squeezed. The pain in Latisha's voice was obvious.

"I'm sorry." Jonas' voice was gruff as he laid a hand on the older woman's shoulder.

She smiled at him. "I suspect you two are newly mated, so don't let this get you down. He had his faults, as do I, but I loved that man for most of my life. I sort of lost a year of myself when he passed. I existed without really living. My children came to visit, tried to talk me into moving in with them, but I couldn't bring myself to make any changes to the life we'd had together."

Cindy's throat burned at the love and grief she witnessed. She couldn't even let herself think about the possibility of losing Jonas.

"Finally, after a while, I started to come back to myself. To look around. I realized I was still living, and there was nothing to be gained by my acting otherwise. My children had lost their father, they didn't need to lose their mother, too."

She paused. "Jonas, would you mind fetching an old lady a beer?"

"Not a bit, Miss Latisha." He brushed his lips over her cheek and hurried off.

"Oh, he's a smooth one all right."

"I don't know, you're the one who's already made him fall in love with you," Cindy pointed out with a grin.

Latisha just winked at her as Jonas returned with a beer for her and a hard lemonade for Cindy.

When she'd taken a couple of sips, Latisha sighed. "My kids were asking me to move in with them, or at least nearby. But they'd both joined other packs, one in Northern California and one in Florida. How was I supposed to choose?"

"No favorites, huh?" Jonas asked.

Latisha backhanded his arm lightly. "They're both good kids. Both have good mates. Good packs. Well, one I had no interest in joining, truth be told, but the other...it's a good pack, but it just wasn't meant to be my new home. I knew it. Just like I knew it was time to move on. I didn't want to be in the place we'd raised our family together. Be there alone, I mean. Even though my pack is great, and I have some family out there, it's too easy to lose myself again, in the day-to-day habits I'm so used to."

Jonas stiffened beside Cindy, enough that Latisha noticed and paused.

He looked at Cindy, who assumed that meant that Brenda had entered the room. How he'd known it was her, she couldn't guess, but it didn't matter.

She touched the other woman's arm. "Please, we want to hear the rest."

Latisha eyed them speculatively, then nodded. "Well, when I heard about this new pack, I thought why not come and take a look?"

"And what you do think so far?" Jonas asked.

"Well, so far I've really only talked to you two, so I'm not quite ready to judge yet."

The twinkle in her eye said differently, and Jonas grinned. "Aw, come on, you know you want to join us. Let me introduce you to my parents. They'll convince you to stay."

"They don't want the honor of being the oldest members of the pack?" Latisha guessed.

"Exactly."

Cindy shook her head, amused at their byplay. "First, why don't we check out the food table. There's some good stuff there, if I do say so myself."

"Jonas said you put this whole thing together," Latisha said as they made their way to the food. "It's beautifully done. So colorful and cheerful."

"Thank you so much. I had help getting it all put up. And help with the food. You have to try these cranberry and brie crostini. They're a new recipe I was trying and they turned out really well."

She didn't have to try to track Brenda through the house, all she needed to do was watch Jonas, as he kept an awareness of the woman. She tugged on his sleeve, then gave him an exasperated look. "Leave it alone."

Bill and Joe came up to the table to get plates of food, and Cindy introduced them to Latisha. She needed to meet more people, and give the rest of the pack a chance to get to know the wonderful woman. She glanced around the room to see Adam and Thomas talking to two young ladies, and Olivia and Tasha talking to a woman who appeared to be about Cindy's age. Candace and Robert were chatting with the Changs. Jen and Myra were talking to Brenda, so Cindy nudged Jonas. "Why don't you go talk to her, see what you think? I'll save her for later, and you can get an idea of her without me there to color it."

He frowned at her, but didn't reply. Trying to decide what was best for her, she knew.

"Seriously, I think that would be smartest. I'm going to go see who's talking to Olivia and Tasha."

"Fine."

She pulled lightly at his shirt, drawing him down to her. "Open mind," she whispered almost soundlessly.

He kissed her. "Fine."

Letting him go, because this time he sounded like he meant it, mostly, Cindy headed over to the Keoghs.

They introduced her to Janet, a banker from outside of Boston. It only took about three minutes for Cindy to decide that Olivia and Tasha weren't fans of Janet's, and two more to decide she felt the same. But she determined to give it more time than that, to try to see past her instinctual dislike.

Olivia excused herself and Tasha to go meet more people, and Cindy asked Janet about her career.

She managed to keep one eye on Jonas, and was pleased that he seemed to be relaxed and genial as he talked to Brenda. It was also great to see the pack doing exactly as they'd been asked, flowing around the room, taking time to meet with each visitor. Adam came to meet Janet, and Cindy moved along to meet Becky and Soo Park.

"I hear you ladies were just mated recently as well. Did you meet my Jonas?" She pointed him out, getting a small wave from him and Tasha, who had joined him.

"We did, and not yet," Soo said, her excitement shining in her eyes. "Isn't being mated the most amazing thing?"

"It's awesome," Cindy agreed. "You know it will be—your whole life, you know—but then it happens, and you realize you had absolutely no idea."

Becky laughed. "That is a perfect description. What is it that you do, Cindy?"

She told them about her blog, and Becky was excited to check it out. "Now that we're mated, we feel like we should probably get around to figuring out that whole adulting thing. I still have some student-loan debt I should have buckled down on, and Soo is driving a car that's about to fall apart, and we have no savings."

"Hey, I love my car!"

"Yeah, but it doesn't love you back, and it's going to kick the bucket within a year, I guarantee it."

"Hmph."

"Well, take a look at the articles, and feel free to ask me if you have any questions, whether you guys end up moving to New Mexico or not."

"So, tell us all about the new pack," Soo demanded.

She did, enjoying the conversation and proud of herself for keeping her focus on the ladies, not anything else that was happening in the living room. When she noticed Jonas heading in another direction, and Brenda moving to talk to Joe, she figured it was time. She worked her way over to them and met Brenda's smile with one of her own.

"Brenda, it's been so long. How was your trip out here?"

"Cindy, it's so good to see you. I met your charming and gorgeous Jonas. You're a lucky girl."

"No question," Cindy agreed. "So, you're considering small-town living?"

Brenda shrugged. "I like to be open to new opportunities. I've been living in the same place for a long time, and this seemed like a good time to explore. Although, I have to admit, it's smaller than I'd realized. And I'm not used to a pack only having one house and a tiny bit of land to its name."

She gestured vaguely at the room, and Cindy took it as Brenda being as unimpressed with the house as she was with the town. But maybe she was projecting.

"Actually, this is a rental. The pack doesn't own anything." *Yet*, she didn't add.

"Tell me about your work, Brenda," Joe said. "Is it something that can be transferred to a new location?"

Brenda nodded. "I'm in insurance, so I should be fine. But that's going to be one of the tougher aspects of getting this pack going, isn't it? It's a lot to ask a small town like this to support as many new people as you need." She looked at Cindy sympathetically. "Jonas mentioned he hadn't found new work yet."

Joe's eyebrows winged up, and Cindy was speechless. She wondered if Jonas had misled Brenda, or if Brenda had misinterpreted something he'd said. It didn't appear to matter, as Brenda continued on.

"But I was so happy to meet Olivia, and learn that the truck stop job seems to be perfect for her."

"Yes, being a manager of a large staff seems to fit perfectly in her wheelhouse," Joe agreed. "Cindy, Bill is over at the food table, and he's trying to catch your attention."

She glanced over and found that Bill was holding up an empty platter. Laughing, she motioned for a minute and turned back to Brenda. "I'm sure we'll have more time to catch up later."

Walking off before the other woman had a chance to respond, she headed to Bill. "Jonas swears there was a backup platter of the spinach dip bites."

"There was. Did you look in the kitchen?" she asked.

"Without your help?" He gave her blank face for a solid five seconds before cracking into a smile.

"Is this because I was talking to Brenda?" she asked.

"Hmm?" He managed to look innocent and intrigued at the same time. He was full of baloney.

She shook her head, linked her arm in his and headed for the kitchen. "We were having a perfectly pleasant conversation. Does *everyone* know that we have history?"

"I mean, it's always hard to keep things from a pack, but when your pack is a grand total of twelve, it's downright impossible."

"Hmm, I guess. Did you talk to her? Never mind, don't tell me, I don't want to know your opinion yet."

"She told me she was impressed that I was bold enough to carry off this sweater so well."

He said it so dryly, she wasn't sure if he was making it up or not. She stopped, examined his very nice cashmere sweater with large black and green horizontal stripes.

"Seriously?"

"Seriously. She seemed to think she was being quite charming."

"Wow."

They entered the kitchen, and of course found the tray of yummy artichoke and spinach dip cooked into little pastry cups right where she'd left them, in plain sight, available to anyone who wanted to grab them. She slanted a look at Bill, who just smiled and picked up the tray.

"You, go talk to people," she told Bill. "I'm going to check in with Myra."

"Yes, ma'am," he barked and marched the tray to the food table.

She smiled as she scanned the room, spotting her best friend talking with Jonas' mom. Excellent, she hadn't yet had a chance to chat with Candace. The woman gave her a warm hug when she reached the pair.

"Hello, darling." Candace kept her hands on Cindy's shoulders, nudging her back so she could take a good look. "How are you doing?"

Cindy sighed. "I'm fine, except for the part where people are worried about me for no good reason."

"A very good reason. Because we love you."

"It's not like we're enemies or anything. We've never even said a cross word to each other."

"And that's why no one is going to treat her badly in this house. Unless she does something now, of course," Myra assured her.

Cindy opened her mouth to respond, but Myra apparently thought it was time to change the subject.

"The party turned out amazing, thank you for all your hard work. All of the food is delicious, but the Sriracha deviled eggs were amazing. What was that sprinkled on top of them?"

Cindy rolled her eyes but let the conversation be diverted. Besides, she was pretty happy with how the menu had turned out and wanted the feedback. "Garlic panko crumbs."

Candace shook her head. "Those were good, but they had nothing on the crab-stuffed mushrooms. I definitely want that recipe. I know you'll be putting it on your blog eventually, but I don't want to wait."

"Family never has to wait," Cindy promised. "I'll send you the recipe tomorrow."

"You're a good girl. And you have good teeth." She leaned in close to Myra and Cindy. "I was not impressed with Brenda's teeth."

For a moment, Cindy could only stare. And then she remembered Candace was a dentist, and she started laughing, Myra right there with her.

"Oh, Candace, you're the best."

She felt Jonas with their bond, a moment before his arms wrapped around her waist and his chin came to rest on top of her head. He loved to hold her like this, she'd come to realize. And she loved it to. She leaned back into him.

"Entertaining my girl pretty well, I see. Thanks, Mom."

"Anything for my boy."

"I've been informed by three out of four of our hierarchy that you are barred from cleanup duty. They said as soon as you're done with the party, we're to leave and let the others handle dismantling and cleaning up. Luckily, since I helped, and I drove with you, I get to leave, too."

"Oh, that's not necessary."

"Make that four out of four of your hierarchy," Myra put in.

Cindy glared at her best friend. "Myra. You know I like to pack the party stuff away." Carefully. To be sure it could be used again.

"I know. I know how you like it done, too, so I can see to that. Besides, tell me right now what your plan is for all the decorations."

"I'm going to donate them to the senior center. I talked to a wonderful lady there, and she said she'd be thrilled to take the decorations anytime I wanted to donate. She was very excited when I brought her the football stuff the other day."

"Right. So you're giving the stuff away, which means if it's not packed exactly how you like it, it makes no difference. But, I still promise to pack it up exactly how you like it."

"Hmph."

"I think you've been outmaneuvered, my dear," Candace said. "And you certainly deserve to go home and rest after all the work you did here. I'll help as well, and Myra can show me what you like, so that in the future, more people can handle that part of things."

"Um…"

She didn't manage more as Jonas squeezed her again. "Why don't we start with the goodbyes?"

"Well, I can see when I'm not wanted anymore," she teased. "Seriously, though, thank you."

"Don't be silly. You don't thank us, we thank you. The party was wonderful, everyone had a good time. I'm really proud of the whole pack for doing what we asked and speaking to all the visitors." Myra said. "But now it's time to send those visitors home. Let's make the rounds!"

Following their alpha's directive, Cindy and Jonas gave his mother hugs. Cindy turned to see who else was nearby and saw Olivia talking to Jen. The conversation looked deep enough that she decided not to interrupt, and save them for last. They made their rounds, had words with all the visitors and hugs with all the pack members, closing it out with Jen and Olivia.

By the time she made it to the car, Cindy collapsed into her seat. "Okay. I didn't realize quite how done I was."

"You should listen to your alpha. And your mate."

"Yeah, yeah, whatever." She was leaning back against the head-rest, eyes closed, but she rolled her head towards him anyway. "It went really well, right? I wasn't just imagining that?"

"It went really well. Our pack acted like a pack and some of the visitors will definitely receive invitations to join. And at least some of them will accept."

She couldn't quite suppress a yawn. "I want to hear all about your impressions."

"Mmm-hmm."

CHAPTER NINE

Jonas couldn't resist frequent glances at his sleeping mate, though he had to be careful on the dark drive home. He had precious cargo. He'd seen her working on the party plans, even helped put it all together, but he was still amazed at the end result.

He'd watched her off and on all night. She was a sociable person, and worked hard at making easy conversation with those who weren't such naturals at it. Most extroverts weren't so great at that, he'd noticed.

When he turned the car off, she mumbled.

"What was that?"

"The job."

She blinked her eyes open and stared at him.

"The job?" he asked.

"Huh?"

"Were you talking in your sleep? You asked me about a job."

She scrubbed her hands over her face. "Oh. Sorry. I really did fall asleep, didn't I?"

"Yep. Sit there, I'll just be a second."

She frowned at him so he pecked a quick kiss on her lips before getting out of the car. He hurried around and opened her door before she could figure out that she was just sitting there doing nothing.

She blinked at him some more. "Hmph."

"Right." He held out his hand, curling it around hers when she accepted his offer. He gave a little tug and pulled her out of the car. In the next move, he lifted her off her feet and into his arms. He waited for her reaction.

"If you think I'm going to complain, you're wrong." She snuggled into him.

"Good." He dropped a kiss on her forward and walked to the door. It wasn't exactly easy, but he thought he managed to unlock and open the door with a minimum of awkwardness and a modicum of sexy romance hero. Her twinkling eyes suggested otherwise, but she didn't say anything, so he didn't either.

He set her down on the bed and went about the task of getting her naked. He was proud of himself for remembering to start with her shoes. Luckily they were just slip-ons. "Now, what was that about a job?"

"Hm? Oh, that. I was wondering what you told Brenda about you working."

He waited for her to lift her butt, then pulled her slacks down. "Well, she asked me if I was working, and I said not yet. Then she asked me what I was looking for, and I said nothing, yet."

"That was it?"

"Pretty much word for word. Why?"

"When I talked to her, she said something like you mentioning you hadn't been able to find work yet."

He'd been unbuttoning her blouse but stopped at that. "Seriously?"

"Yep. With this sweet, sympathetic tone."

He snorted. "Well, the good news is, I don't think you have to be worried about anyone wanting to offer her a place in our pack. Nobody seemed to be impressed with her. And," he said, holding up a hand to stop her from interrupting him, "I truly believe everyone did give her a chance."

She shrugged out of the top. "Okay. If you say so, then I'll believe it and let it go. Without guilt."

"Believe it." He leaned forward and kissed her forehead.

"Nope."

"Nope?"

"Nope with that forehead nonsense, I seem to be finding my second wind."

"Is that right?" He trailed a finger down her neck, across her shoulder. "You were pretty tired a minute ago."

"True, but then my sexy mate got me naked. He should go about getting himself naked, now, too."

"You think so?" He trailed his finger from her hip to the side of her breast, watching as her nipple started to pucker, though he wasn't really close to it.

"I do," she sighed. "I definitely think so."

"Whatever you say." He stopped touching her, backed away. She watched him closely. She might have even whimpered. He had excellent hearing, but he wasn't certain.

He unbuttoned his own shirt, not hurrying, but not going slowly, either. When he took it off and tossed it to the floor, her gaze never moved from his body. His tidy mate was definitely in the mood if she was ignoring him tossing his clothes on the floor.

His belt soon followed, then his pants. He stepped forward so he was at the end of the bed. "Come here, woman."

"I'm right here."

"I thought you had your second wind?"

"That means I need to come to you? Why don't you come over here?"

"I'll help," he offered, and snaked a hand out to grab her ankle.

She alternated between a shriek and a laugh as he hauled her to the end of the bed. He tugged her up until she was on her knees, then he teased her with darting kisses until she grew frustrated, grabbed his head in her hands, and kissed him for all she was worth. Just as he liked it.

He pulled her tight against him, her soft skin pressed into his aching dick. She raked her nails up his back, tiny claws digging in, spurring him on. It took a while, but he finally tore free from her kisses.

"Turn around." It came out as a bit of a growl, but she didn't seem to mind. She turned, then immediately looked over her should to give him a saucy grin. Damn, he loved this woman.

He set his hand on her ass and ran it slowly up her back, pushing her down. She teased him with token resistance, but lowered until she was braced on her elbows. He caressed her beautiful ass, and she wiggled it at him. He bit back a laugh and tested her wetness.

"So wet for me, baby. I guess you really do have your second wind."

He speared two fingers into her.

"Told you," she panted.

He couldn't resist the temptation, so he leaned in and bit her butt cheek.

"Hey!" she cried out, but leaned back into him for more.

"Hold still now," he said, fitting himself at her entrance. Her slick heat beckoned him, inviting him to thrust in hard and fast. An invitation he was happy to accept.

She cried out as he buried himself deep within her channel. He leaned over her, kissing his way up her back. She rose until her arms were straight, bringing her neck within reach. He sucked and nipped, not moving inside her until she was calling his name.

"Jonas, please. I need you, Jonas."

He braced one hand on the bed beside her and brought the other to her hip, holding on as he began to pump in and out, in and out, until he couldn't think of anything except her sweet, sweet, heat. She came apart underneath him, around him, clenching tight as he fought to move. Dropping back down to her elbows, she moaned his name one more time.

Standing up straight again, both hands on her hips, he slowed down, gave one last furious thrust, and released within her. "Cindy. Fuck! So sweet."

She looked back at him, her expression pure bliss and love. "Need help lying down?"

He laughed, pulled free from her, eliciting another gasp. Putting his hands under her, he helped her back to the top of the bed, then fumbled to get the covers down so they could get underneath. "Maybe we need to plan this out better next time."

"I think it worked out just fine." Her voice was sleepy again as she snuggled in next to him. "What did you think of the other visitors tonight?"

"You want me to talk right now? With logic and thought?"

She giggled. Not a sound he heard from her often, so he memorized it now.

"I liked Becky and Soo a lot. Janet, not so much."

"Agreed."

"The Changs would be great, especially for Tasha."

"Yup."

"You already know that if we weren't mated, I'd be asking Miss Latisha if I could move in with her."

Another giggle. He was going to have to get her this tired more often, if this was his reward.

"You should get some sleep," he told her.

"Yeah. But I like this. Building our pack. It was great tonight. It felt like we were a real pack, for the first time."

He might have answered, but instead he just smiled when her breathing evened out into sleep.

"You know who makes the best breakfasts?" Cindy asked when Jonas had barely opened his eyes.

"Um. Not me in the next ten minutes, I hope."

"Truckers."

"Truckers?" He frowned, tried to engage his brain.

"Truck drivers. Well, not truckers. They might not make the best breakfasts. But they eat them. So we should go to the truck stop for breakfast."

Ah. Okay. He glanced at the clock. Seven was a perfectly reasonable time to wake up and have breakfast. "Right. Good plan. Wait, it's Sunday, would Olivia be working?"

"She told me she was going to go in for a half day, just while she's getting a feel for the place and all the people. But I think not until eight."

"Perfect. We'll shower, call Tasha, see if she wants to join us."

She made no move to get up. He did not attempt to change that.

"What do you have planned for the day?" she asked.

"There was that parcel of land we saw online the other day. We could go check it out."

"That's an excellent idea. And we can drive around, see if anything else catches our eye. After breakfast?"

"Perfect."

She was tracing patterns on his chest again. A spiral and a J, if he had to guess.

"It's a good plan," she said, after a few more minutes.

"Yes."

She still didn't move, and he couldn't keep from laughing.

He got up, slung her over his shoulder, and headed to the shower with her smacking his ass.

They managed to share the shower and not take *too* long with other activities. While she dried her hair, he answered a text from Adam. He waited until she was done with the dryer and gave her the update.

"Adam texted to say he's supposed to come talk to us and find out our thoughts on the visitors. I told him he could meet us for breakfast, come for dinner, or we could just tell him in five seconds what our thoughts are."

"Which are?"

"Janet and Brenda are no, everyone else is yes."

"Okay, yeah, I guess it is that easy. What did he opt for?"

"He's meeting us at the truck stop. Said he's been wanting to check it out, too."

They were on their way in short order, having decided not to be stupid adults who called a teenager at eight on a Sunday morning.

When they got to the cafe attached to the truck stop, they asked a waitress where they could find the manager. Her look was highly suspicious as she went to a phone, keeping her gaze on them the whole time she spoke. It wasn't any less negative when she told them Mrs. Keogh would be a couple of minutes, and they could go ahead and take a seat in the diner.

Jonas was still debating on which greasy breakfast he was going to want, while being impressed that the menu also offered a selection of healthier options, when both Adam and Olivia joined them.

"We don't want to interrupt your work, we just wanted to say hi and check the place out. We haven't been here before," Cindy told her.

"I can sit a minute. Have you ordered? The food is pretty good, as long as you're expecting truck stop diner food."

"That's exactly what we're hoping for," Jonas assured her.

They gave their orders to the waitress, who had been watching for a signal from Olivia.

"We were going to ask Tasha if she wanted to come, too, but then it occurred to us that waking her up on a weekend wouldn't really endear her to us."

"She does like to sleep in on a Sunday." She grinned. "I told her when I get home we can go driving around, explore the area."

"We'll be doing that a bit, as well, after breakfast. We'll have to compare notes later," Cindy told her.

"Definitely." Olivia turned towards Adam. "You said you wanted to ask me about my impressions from the party later, but since you're here, can't we just talk now?"

"I wanted you to be able to talk in private."

Olivia frowned. "I can't think of anything I would tell you that I'm not perfectly happy to say in front of Cindy and Jonas. I only have a few minutes, but unless you have a lot of questions for me, it won't take long to tell you that I liked everyone except Janet and Brenda. I found them both to be fairly negative." She sighed. "And I know that's hypocritical of me, as I can be—*have* been—fairly negative, so if the pack decides to invite them to join, I'm completely fine with that, and will make it a point to spend some time getting to know them and hoping that there's a reason for their negativity."

"Ditto," Jonas said.

"Exactly," Cindy said.

"Fair enough," Adam said. "Let's eat," he suggested as the waitress brought the three meals to the table.

Olivia seemed surprised that there was no further reaction to her statement, but Adam had moved on, telling Cindy again how much he'd enjoyed the food at the party.

They chatted for a few minutes, and when Cindy asked about how she was finding the work, Olivia said she actually needed to get back to it, so they said their goodbyes and tucked into their eggs.

"Myra and I are thinking things have progressed well enough that it seems likely we'll stay in Alicante," Adam said after he'd eaten half his breakfast. "What do you guys think?"

"It feels right to me. We'll always have to consider the difficulty of jobs, but that's going to be true of any of the small towns we try, and I don't feel like we should be a big-city pack."

"What she said," Jonas added.

Adam nodded "We're going to start looking around at real estate. Sounds like you guys already decided the same."

"Yes," Cindy said. "We've seen one place we like okay, but don't totally love. We're going to try out another today. If I remember correctly—"

"Which, of course, she does," Jonas interrupted.

"—there are a few parcels in the same general area, so one might work for you guys as well."

"Okay, let us know what you think. The rental house works pretty well for a pack house. Joe said he'd consider moving in if we get our own place."

"He'd be great at running the pack house," Cindy said.

"And since the house is out on the edge of town, some of the land that butts up to it hasn't been developed. I'm going to check into the properties, see if maybe we can talk some owners into selling."

"That would be awesome. The spot we're going to look at first is pretty close to there." Cindy wiped up the last of the egg yolk with her bread. "And I'm definitely adding this place to my list of possible job opportunities for new pack members."

"Speaking of lists," Jonas said. "Do you have one about what we need to do to get married? I'm assuming you don't want a wedding, since you haven't said anything, but I should probably ask, just to be sure. But we should get official in the eyes of the government."

She laughed. "No, I'm good without a wedding—and yes, I have a list for the steps we need to take to get married. I'll show you tonight. I have a mental note that the next time either of us goes to the city, we need to check a couple of things off that list."

"Gotcha."

They drank some coffee with Adam then said their goodbyes. Cindy drove back towards the pack house, then a ways past it. When she'd parked, she grabbed a printout and walked him about fifty yards before studying the paper and nodding. "I think this is it."

Jonas took the paper but didn't look at it, instead looking around at the land and the view. "Okay. Our house is about two miles that way," he pointed. "And there's the pack house, over there. Right?"

"Right."

"Nice view."

"Nice enough for a house?"

He did a slow three-sixty. "A lot of work. A lot of lists," he teased. But his gut was telling him they were in the right spot. She took his hand and squeezed.

"I could make building us a house my focus, instead of deciding on a new job. Get us settled."

"You shouldn't have to do the bulk of the work if you don't want to. We can hire people for that. Thomas is a contractor, right?"

"I think I would enjoy it. Working with an architect, and yeah, still with a contractor. I'm not claiming I can do that job. But it will be a lot less stressful for both of us, I think, if we're not trying to squeeze it in around two full-time jobs."

He turned in a circle, then moved along for a different view. "We'd be able to make all the decisions to get the perfect place for us. Give you an office with a view, since that's where you spend most of your day. An awesome porch, so we can sit and watch the stars."

"Then that's what we'll do." She went up on her toes, but he met her more than halfway, and kissed her softly.

"How much land, again?" he asked. He glanced at the paper he was holding.

"It's only twenty acres, but all that land there," she pointed, "is protected. No building, no camping. For four hundred acres."

"So we'd have all that land to run on."

"Exactly. And where this land ends, over there," she pointed, "is the other parcel of forty acres, which we can go look at too. The views look like they would be pretty similar. If we don't have a huge preference for the specific land, I'll vote for the smaller parcel for us, and the see if Myra and Adam might like the larger."

"Agreed."

"We don't have to decide now. These parcels have been up for sale for quite a while."

"We'll go take a look, but my bet's on that plan. Even if Myra and Adam aren't sold on it, this is perfect for us." He kissed her. "I'll look into finding us a realtor. Or do you already have a list?"

She laughed. "Of course I do. And I'm happy to hand it over."

CHAPTER TEN

Cindy hit the *publish* button on her screen and sat back in her chair with a sigh. It had been an intense article to research and write, but an important one. She'd had articles about insurance and wills before, but this one went deeper. And reminded her that she needed to put a priority on getting their marriage handled. Just because they, and the pack, considered mates to be spouses, didn't mean the government would agree. Her current will put her assets in her brother's hands, so she could trust that he would hand things over to Adam, but it would be unnecessarily complicated. A marriage license would fix that. And they both needed new wills.

She stretched and moved back up to the keyboard. Pulling up the list she'd already started, she dove into it, researching marriage licenses for their county to start with. She kept an eye on the clock. Jonas had told her he was going to help out at the pack house for a while.

The living room, kitchen and dining room had been set up, but now they needed to make the rest of the house into a home, ready for visitors and any pack members who might choose to live there before setting up their own houses. Plus, they needed to make it a space where the kids could hang out if their parents weren't home, or they just wanted to socialize with each other.

He'd said he thought they would start painting the bedrooms today. Since she'd finished her work early enough, she could make the more complicated of the two dinners she'd tentatively planned. She pulled up the to-do list for today, confirmed she hadn't missed anything, crossed out her Plan B dinner option, marked her work as done, and closed the list. She pulled out her phone, switched from her working playlist to one of her cooking playlists, and turned on the speakers for the whole house.

Instead of heading to the kitchen, she went to the bedroom and pulled out an apron she'd ordered last week and hidden in her drawer. It was retro style, bold red with large white polka dots. It boasted a lacy sweetheart neckline and a thick, sassy white tie around the waist. It was completely ridiculous, and she loved it, and was sure that Jonas would too. Especially over her cozy yoga pants and the long-sleeve thermal she was wearing.

She danced and chopped, sang and twirled, photographed and planned. When she had achieved a simmer, she turned to drinks. A little tug on the mate bond told her that Jonas was in a good, happy mood. Probably a little bit tired from the day's work, but not too much. She considered her options. Making something that would bring a smile to his face was priority number one. Having that something be a recipe that could be posted on her blog was just a bonus.

Pulling out her phone, she accessed her file of possibilities and explored. Hmm, an Old Fashioned? A Gibson? No, not after a day of painting. A Mojito? Ah, a Tom Collins. Perfect.

She pulled out everything she needed and prepped the garnishes, then took pictures. She checked along her bond and didn't sense Jonas on the move, so she figured she had some time to check in with Myra.

Myra answered on the first ring. "Tell me everything."

Cindy laughed. "Nothing's happening here, I just wanted to

check in with you. I figured inviting and rejecting was probably a stressful process."

"Well, you're not wrong. I'm so glad I have Adam to help me out, and of course Jen and Joe have been great as well. Remind me to make sure that any new members of the hierarchy don't have names that start with J."

"Or at least have more than three letters."

"That would work, too. We talked to all of the pack, and decided to invite the Changs, the Parks and Mrs. Bogan."

"That's Miss Latisha to you," Cindy interjected.

Myra's laugh was clear and easy, so Cindy wasn't too worried about the stress of the decisions, and relaxed. She moved to the couch and plopped down.

"Right, Miss Latisha is awesome, and has already accepted our invitation. She's going to take her time with the move, so we might not see her for a couple of months, but she's in."

"Yay!"

"It was basically unanimous on all counts, so there wasn't any reason to talk it out. The Changs had made a whole vacation out of coming out here. I talked to Sofia, and she said that they wanted to wait until the vacation was over and the kids were back to normal life, and then talk to them about it. So we should hear from them in a couple of weeks. But she sounded very excited."

"Excellent. Blaire and Tasha seemed to hit it off pretty well. It will be so much better for Tasha if she has another wolf to be close to."

"Definitely. That was one of the reasons I sent her to Chicago in the first place, they have such a big pack with a wide range of ages."

"It was a good plan. Just because it didn't work, doesn't mean it wasn't a smart play."

"True. I spoke with Becky Park, and she said that she and Soo had liked everyone, but were a little worried about the size of the town. Now that they know they would be accepted, they want to do some more research about where they might be able to work, make sure they can make a real go of it. They're excited to dive into that research and will let us know soon. I told them they should contact you, as you might be able to point them in some good directions."

"Absolutely."

"Adam spoke to both Brenda and Janet."

"How did you decide who would speak to whom?" She had no doubt there'd been a debate on that.

"Well, first he got me to agree that one person would call the people we wanted to invite and one person would call those we didn't accept."

"You can say rejected," Cindy said with a laugh. "It's me you're talking to."

"Yeah, yeah, the rejected. So, of course, I said he should do the accepted and I would do the rejected. And, of course, he said *he* would do the rejected."

"Color me shocked," she teased.

"So we flipped a coin. I'm still not convinced he didn't cheat somehow."

"Pretty sure you'd be able to tell if he cheated. What did he say, how did it go?"

"He said Janet told him it didn't matter, as she wasn't interested in joining."

"Uh-huh."

"He said Brenda seemed pretty surprised, but in a trying-to-play-it-cool kind of way."

"That's all he said?" Myra kicked her feet up onto the coffee table.

"He said she was very reserved once she understood what he was saying, and got off the phone pretty quickly."

"I guess that sounds about right. Are you going to tell me how many people recommended invite versus reject on her?"

"Oh please, everyone disliked her. They all mentioned she'd said something that rubbed them the wrong way, if not actively annoyed them."

"You would think she'd be a little more capable when actively trying to get people to like her."

"You'd think."

Cindy heard a tone through her phone that signaled Myra getting a text. Then her own phone beeped with a message. "You check yours, I'll check mine," she said.

Hers was a message from Jonas asking if she wanted to come have dinner at the pack house. She quickly replied to tell him she was already making dinner for him. He texted back a kissy emoji and said he'd be heading home shortly.

"Hey," she said, when she put the phone back to her ear.

"Hey. Apparently we're having a pizza party here. I guess this is a sign that I should get out of the office and see what's happening in the rest of the house."

"I told Jonas I was already cooking and to get his sexy butt home."

"Nice. You guys have a good dinner. I won't even point out that you didn't invite me."

Cindy laughed. "Didn't even consider it."

"Bitch."

"You know you love me. Did Jonas tell you guys about the land we looked at, and think you should, too?"

"Yep, we drove out this morning. We like the land, for sure, just not sure how interested we are in building from scratch. We're going to do a bit of research, see how complicated that is. But we're definitely interested. And we've confirmed with the landlord for this house that she'd like to sell."

"Excellent. It's all coming together. You guys have fun tonight. Call me tomorrow and tell me all about it."

They said their goodbyes and Cindy checked the time as well as her link to Jonas. He was on his way, she could tell. She switched to a different playlist and danced her way back to the kitchen, made a small pitcher of the Tom Collins, tested it. Delicious. She poured two glasses and added a cherry and slice of orange to each.

When she felt him close, she listened for the car on the driveway, and went to open the door, drink in hand to meet her mate.

AFTER AN AMAZING MEAL, a wonderful time divesting Cindy of her fantastic apron, and a very good night, Jonas woke up refreshed and more than ready to face the day. He kissed his mate and set up with his laptop on the couch. There was a nice chair in her office, but he was pretty sure he wouldn't be able to resist interrupting her a hundred times if he was in there.

He could make out the soft sound of her music from down the hall, and the clicking of her keyboard. She was a bit hard on the poor thing, he was fascinated to discover. Maybe he should consider investing in a keyboard company.

After researching her list of realtors for a while, he settled on a couple he liked, made some calls. Then he made some sandwiches and stuck his head in her office.

"Baby, I made sandwiches. Ham and cheddar. You want one now, or I can leave it in the kitchen for you later?"

She looked up from her monitor and stared at him for a second before adjusting her brain. Then she checked the clock and smiled. "I'll eat with you."

She joined him in the living room, where he'd already set out a soft drink for her.

"I checked the realtors. There are two in the city that I liked. We could go out there when you have an afternoon, meet with them, have a nice restaurant dinner, and come back. Should be about a forty-five minute drive."

"Right, that's where the Target is. And the county clerk's office."

He laughed. "Exactly."

She took a couple of bites and pulled her phone out to check her schedule. "What are the chances both of them have tomorrow free?"

"Chances are excellent, as of an hour ago. One isn't available the next day, the other not available on Friday, but other than that, they're pretty open."

"Jeez, let's not go into the real estate business."

"Good plan. Not in this area, at least."

"I can totally make tomorrow work."

He leaned in to kiss her. "I'll set it up. And find a restaurant that looks good."

She cocked her head. "I'm so used to doing all the planning and organizing for my life. I kind of worried that a mate would just be more work for me. But you make things so easy."

"I aim to please. Besides, talk about easy. You make dinner more than half the time. You make an amazing cocktail. And you buy aprons just to make me crazy."

"That's true. We're pretty awesome together."

He helped Jen with a project at her house the next morning, made quesadillas for lunch, and packed Cindy into the car in plenty of time to swing by the clerk's office before their afternoon appointment with the first realtor.

Two meetings later, they made it to the seafood restaurant.

"So, what did you think?" she asked, after they'd ordered.

"Number one was okay, but I liked number two better. She seemed pretty sharp."

"And more used to working on deals well outside of town, though I don't know how much of a difference that might make."

"I'll email her in the morning. Mom and Dad invited us over for dinner tomorrow, if you feel like it. They want to try some recipes that they've been working on."

"Sounds fun. Does that mean they're committing to opening up some kind of food establishment?"

"Nope. They're still just in a testing phase."

"That's cool, no reason to hurry. Your mom mentioned teeth at the party, maybe she'll go back to being a dentist."

"I actually told her she should consider it, when I realized the closest dentist is twenty minutes outside of town. She could work one day a week, if she wanted to. Even less. One or two days a month. She did always enjoy being a dentist, but in her head, it's a full-time gig."

They bantered with the waitress when she brought water, letting her know they needed some time to look at the menu. When the young woman had left, Cindy leaned towards him. "I think we should send Joe here for dinner sometime when she's working."

"Think so, huh? Still feeling the romance in the air?"

"With you around, I feel it every day." She batted her eyelashes at him.

He managed not to snort. She was damn cute. "Have you ever guessed someone's mate, when meeting a stranger? What are the chances of that?"

"I'm not saying she's his mate, but he could certainly enjoy himself for a while."

He raised his glass to her in acknowledgment. He'd certainly enjoyed himself with a few women over the years, knowing full well they weren't his mate, but he had no intentions of having that conversation with her.

"Have you talked to Jen to see how her first few days went?" he asked, changing the subject.

"No, I tried earlier today, but I missed her. I did talk to Adam, who talked to her briefly, and he said so far, so good."

When the food arrived, it proved to be delicious. He tried her salmon and she tried his shrimp scampi, but they each preferred their own dish. They'd opted for a bottle of wine, so when they left, Jonas suggested they walk around for a bit before getting in the car.

She held on to his arm as they walked, something he loved. They explored one side of the block, then crossed the street to come back up the other side.

"Mm, I love this song," she said as they passed a bar.

They heard cheering and looked at each other. "Shall we see what's up?" he asked.

"Sure."

They went inside, and he spotted a table and headed for it, while Cindy pointed at a banner declaring Turtle Racing. He had to read it twice to make sure he understood what it said, then he busted out laughing.

"Wow, we have to see this." He swerved around the table he'd been aiming for and moved toward the small crowd ringed around a large raised table.

A woman in a shirt with the bar logo on it was setting two turtles into a ring in the center of the table. She turned and received two more turtles from someone else and added them to the ring. Most of the table was painted with a light blue circle that was about sixty inches in diameter. Beyond the circle, the table was painted red. The turtles had stickers on top of their shells. Superman, Batman, Spider-Man and Iron Man. At the edge of the table were two men and two women, each holding one superhero emblem.

The woman who'd handled the turtles put her hand on the barrier ring while someone behind her counted down.

"Three...two...one...go!"

She lifted the ring, and the turtles—did nothing. For a second. Or three. Then Batman made a break, but turned into his fellow turtles, so didn't make much progress. However, that prompted the others to start moving. Superman had some speed, but didn't seem to have the hang of a straight line. Spider-Man was slow, but was making steady progress towards the red. Iron Man started chasing after Superman. Batman had turned around again and was basically still in the center.

Spiderman was close, one of the guys yelling his encouragement, but then he veered off three inches from the red. Superman was closing in, earning a clapping cheer from one of the ladies. The other spectators started chanting, "Go, go, go!"

Spider-Man's trajectory was heading him back to the line at an angle, but then he turned again, and was there. He hit the red, and the whole group exploded into cheers.

Cindy was laughing, so beautiful he had to interrupt her for a kiss. She didn't seem to mind and smiled at him when he pulled back.

"Do you want a drink? And do you want to sponsor a turtle?"

"Yes and yes. Let's go to the bar."

They made their way over. The place had plenty of people inside, but it wasn't crowded. She ordered a hard cider and he got a soda. They paid the fee and received their sign, which had Black Panther on it. They made their way back to the racing table. Thor, Aquaman, Wonder Woman and Deadpool were about to race. They cheered the turtles on and congratulated the guy next to them when his Deadpool was first to cross the line.

They were up next. He checked the competitors and leaned in close so Cindy could hear him. "The Hulk might be a problem, he looks wily."

"Catwoman's bigger than the others. That might give her an edge."

"Captain America is always a contender. But I have faith in our Black Panther."

They joined with the crowd in calling out the countdown. "Three…two…one…go!"

Their turtle made a good start, but then circled for no apparent reason. The Hulk nudged Captain America out of the way, but then sort of stopped. Catwoman was making a perfect trajectory towards the line, but moving very, very slowly. Black Panther resumed course and headed towards the red. The Hulk started back up, but Captain America was getting close, too. Catwoman was on track, but still a couple of inches short. Black Panther veered again, and Jonas and Cindy both groaned.

"Come on, baby, you can do it!" Cindy called out.

Captain America decided to circle. Catwoman was still on target. The Hulk stepped it up and bumped into Black Panther, knocking them both off target as Catwoman slowly made her way right over the line.

The guy with the Catwoman sign whooped and cheered as the crowd congratulated him.

Laughing, they abandoned the races and found a two-top table to relax at while they finished their drinks.

CHAPTER ELEVEN

Cindy finished her cider and considered another round of turtle racing, but decided she'd rather head home. She raised an eyebrow at Jonas, and he gave a little head jerk towards the door, so she knew they were in sync. She took the hand he held out and they made their way back to his car.

The drive home was pleasant. She was getting used to the astonishing lack of traffic out here, though it was still weird to have to drive forty-five minutes to get to a Target. The radio wasn't getting much reception, so she punched in one of her playlists. She'd been working on discovering which music Jonas had the best reactions to, and had made a list. This was her first time trying it out, and she was pleased to see his fingers tapping along to many of them.

As he neared their driveway, she was surprised to see a car parked in it, next to hers. He glanced at her but she just shrugged.

She gasped when the doors opened and her parents got out of the car.

Jonas pulled to a stop. "What?"

"That's my mom and dad."

"Wow. Okay. Any chance this is a good thing?"

"Slim."

"Do you want to wait here, and I'll get rid of them?"

She sighed. "No. Thanks, but no. Let's find out what's happening."

She got out and met Jonas at the front of the car. "Mom, Dad, hi. Meet Jonas. Jonas, my mom, Dana and my dad, Tom."

Jonas held a hand out to her mother, who seemed reluctant, but then took it. Her father followed suit then looked expectantly at Cindy.

"Let's go inside." She gestured towards the front door, and then led the way.

"Since we've been waiting for hours, that would seem to be the thing to do," her father said.

"Did I somehow miss the fact that you guys were coming to our house today? Or even this state?" Cindy asked as she opened the door and held it wide.

"We texted you hours ago."

"Okay. Well, we were in meetings and then a restaurant, so I had my ringer off. But it takes more than several hours to get here, so I'm confused as to why I didn't know you were coming." She hated the swirl of acid in her stomach, because she knew she shouldn't let them get to her. *Knew* she had done nothing wrong.

They all stood in the entryway and Jonas pointed towards the living room. She considered offering them drinks, and decided no. Her parents perched on the edge of the love seat as if it would swallow them hole. She and Jonas sat on the couch and waited.

"We've come to tell you we're ashamed of your actions, and we *insist* that you correct your behavior," her father said.

Her stomach fell and her throat burned. Jonas tensed beside her, but she willed him to stay calm and rested a hand on his leg.

"I have no idea what I could possibly have done that would make you think it's okay to show up at my house and say something like that." She was proud that her words were firm and steady. Her stomach may be roiling, but they didn't need to know that.

"Brenda told us that you went behind her back to make sure she wasn't asked to join the new pack," her mother said, indignation practically dripping from her words.

She shouldn't be surprised. This was completely true to form for them. For whatever reason, they'd always considered her less important than...well, just about anyone else in their world.

"Well, that's actually not true, so if that's all you have, we can probably be done now." Again, she managed to make the words firm and calm, despite feeling neither.

Beside her, Jonas slouched back into the couch, slung one ankle over the other knee, and took her hand in his. He squeezed her hand, a gentle reminder that he had her back, one hundred percent. She tested their link, felt his frustration and determination. Knowing her Jonas, he wanted to step in, throw them out, but was waiting for a cue from her that she would welcome that action. It helped her, steadied her.

"Don't be more rude than you already have been, Cynthia."

"I thought showing up unannounced at someone's house and then accusing them of amoral actions was being rude," Jonas drawled. "But maybe my scale is off."

"Brenda has no reason to lie," her mom said.

"And Cindy does?" Jonas asked.

"We don't know *what* Cindy does out here, or out in St. Louis, but at home, Brenda's a part of our pack. She's hierarchy."

Cindy drew in a deep breath, trying to quell the nausea. "Mom. Dad. I didn't ask the hierarchy not to invite Brenda. They're being selective about who joins, because it's a very new pack, very small, so they're being careful. I can't tell you why they didn't choose to invite Brenda, but it was not at my request." She stood. "If that's all, I think it would be best that you left now."

Jonas stood by her side. "I agree."

"No," her father said firmly. "You've created this mess, and you *will* talk to Myra and fix it."

Her dad was turning red, and her mom was beginning to look less frosty and more...anxious? Cindy sat back down, tugging Jonas with her. She heard a very faint growl from him, but he did as she asked. She rubbed her forehead and tried to make sense of the ridiculous situation.

"If the hierarchy doesn't want Brenda in the pack, there's nothing I can do about that. If I personally thought she'd be a good fit for us, I'd talk to Myra and Adam and give them my opinion about that. But I don't. She's not a nice person, she's not a good leader, and I'm *glad* that they didn't invite her. If they had indicated that they were going to, I also might have offered my opinion. But they didn't, so there was no need for me to say anything."

"You are maligning our fourth. She's already helped your insignificant little pack when she didn't need to, finding that pathetic woman a job," Tom said.

The bite to his words should have had the acid in her stomach shooting up her throat. Instead, it was the opposite. Like a cooling balm, she settled. They weren't just insulting her, but her pack. And her packmate.

Jonas' hand had tightened on hers, and she knew it was costing him to keep the casual air he'd adopted.

"Okay. If I ignore your very rude words regarding my pack and my packmate, I'm left with pointing out that Brenda asked a friend to offer an interview. That's it. It's appreciated, but not all that amazing. And I don't even know why we're having this conversation."

"Brenda would be an asset to any pack," Dana said. "She bends over backwards to help her packmates, like she did with that woman. She helped us when we needed it, and the only thing she's ever asked in return is that we get you to see reason."

Cindy blinked. Her father huffed. Her mom was actually crying now.

It finally occurred to Cindy that this wasn't in the least about her.

She'd been sick with trying to understand why her parents didn't like or respect her, why they thought it was okay to treat her like this, and the answer was so simple. They weren't really thinking about her at all. She was only peripherally involved, as they'd somehow convinced themselves she was keeping them from something they wanted.

And she'd lost her respect for them.

It burned that they had so little for her, but if she didn't respect them in turn, it made it much easier not to give a shit. These people were not important to her. Jonas was. Myra and Adam were. Her pack was.

"I didn't know you had needed help, but I'm glad she was able to give it. I don't see what that has to do with me, though. Why don't you tell me what happened, and we can see if we can figure all of this out."

Dana looked to Tom. He remained tight-lipped and shook his head. "Tom, she's not listening, she's obviously not going to do what we've asked her to. You have to tell her, convince her."

He turned back to Cindy. "I shouldn't have to explain myself to you. If you had any respect for your parents, you would do as you're told."

She started to respond, but he held up his hand. His voice had gotten tighter and rougher, and she could see he was practically vibrating with his anger. Jonas was a solid wall at her side, ready to react in an instant, but she didn't think her father had it in him to be violent. Of course, nothing about this visit made sense, so she appreciated her mate's caution.

"We made some investments with Brenda's firm. They didn't go well. That's what happens with investments, you have to take risks to succeed, but you can't win every time. She helped us out, loaned us the money to cover it and make a new investment. When it comes in, we'll pay her back and be set for retirement. We just need a little more time for it to mature and succeed."

Cindy sat in stunned silence for a full minute.

"So you can see now, right?" Dana asked when she hadn't responded. "How important this is? How you should put aside your petty differences and make the right choice?"

"Okay. Wow. There's a lot to what you just said. Can we start with the fact that you made a very risky investment, with money you apparently didn't have, with your insurance salesperson? Is that right?"

"That's none of your business," Tom insisted.

"Apparently it is," Jonas put in.

"You can stay out of this," Tom said.

"If you want me to stay out of it, you should get out of my house."

"This is Cindy's house, she rented it before she even met you."

Cindy held up her hand. "You're upset and angry, don't add stupid to it. Jonas is my mate, and we need to get back to that fact that you've borrowed money for a high-risk investment. I'm assuming a lot of money, since you think that if it works out, it will set you up for retirement. I know you used to save for retirement. Is that what you used for the first investment?"

"That's none of—"

"Does your alpha know about this?" Jonas asked.

"It's none of—"

"Yeah, not their business, I got it." Jonas just shook his head, looked to Cindy.

She took it to mean that he was ready to shut this down, but was following her lead. "Right, so it sounds like my summary was accurate. And I'll go further. It sounds to me like *Brenda* walked you into both of these investments, when she was supposed to be advising you on your insurance needs. She failed you, and probably scammed you, and instead of acknowledging and dealing with your failures—and hers—you are here badgering *me*. Because she's threatening you to do so. Isn't that extortion?"

Tom stood. "We don't need to be insulted like this."

Cindy and Jonas stood as well. "No, you don't. You can remove yourself from *this* situation and spend some time dealing with the one you've already landed yourself in, instead," Jonas suggested. "I would highly recommend a chat with your alpha, as well."

Dana rose. "I don't know why we thought that you would step up and do the right thing."

"What you don't understand is that I *am* doing the right thing.

But you're so mired in yourselves and looking to blame anyone else, that you don't have a hope of seeing it." She gestured to the front door.

Dana looked like she was going to start ranting, but Tom put his hand on her arm. "It's late and we're out in the middle of nowhere," he said, and gestured out the window. "Are you going to throw us out?"

Jonas finally snapped. A little. Cindy felt how tightly he was holding back. "You can't possibly have expected to stay here."

"This is our daughter's home," Dana snapped.

"Can they stay at the pack house?" Cindy asked Jonas.

He winced. "The paint smell is probably gone by now, but everything's still covered in plastic. Probably wouldn't take too long to get the beds cleaned off and made up—about as much time as it would take them to drive to the motel."

She liked to think she'd come a long way in cutting her parents' negativity from her life in the last half hour, but she still couldn't stand the idea of sending them out this late at night.

"Cindy, I'm asking you if we can please stay the night," Tom said. "We'll leave in the morning and not bother you."

"Tell me what you're proud of her for," Jonas said.

Cindy jerked. She felt a pulse of reassurance down their link.

"You can stay...if you can tell me how she makes you proud to be your daughter."

"That's ridiculous," Dana said.

"And you both have to have an answer, if you both want to stay," he added. "There are motels forty-five minutes away. It's not a bad drive."

"She's our daughter," Tom said.

"Which means what?" Cindy asked.

"Of course we're proud of you."

Cindy just waited. She wasn't sure what had led Jonas to this path, but she trusted that he thought it would help. It certainly couldn't make things worse, at this point.

Tom pulled in a deep breath. Cindy couldn't tell if he had finally realized he'd made a mistake, or if he was considering his options. As Jonas had said, it wouldn't be that difficult for them to drive to the city and get a motel. But Tom seemed hesitant to do that...so maybe there was some chance he was sorry for how things had gone.

"Your brother tells me that the business you've built is impressive. I don't know much about that kind of website, but I know that building something like that from scratch takes a lot of hard work and skill. I'm proud of you."

It shouldn't still matter. Not when she'd just convinced herself that their opinions of her didn't. And she wasn't even sure how sincere he was. But, it did. Her throat tightened, but she managed to nod. "Thank you." She wouldn't give him more than that. He didn't deserve it.

"This is just silly," Dana said. She almost sounded like she might cry. "You're our daughter, of course we're proud of you. Why would you think otherwise?"

Cindy laughed. Actually laughed out loud, to the clear displeasure of her mother.

"Probably because you've done nothing in word or action to show her?" Jonas suggested. "Or, more likely, because your actions have actually shown her the opposite."

"That's not true at all. We've never told you we weren't proud of you."

"In a hundred different ways," Cindy said.

"Of course we're proud of you. You're our daughter," she repeated. "You were a good child, got good grades, and our alpha has mentioned more than once what a boon you are to your pack. I just don't understand why you had to go away and do these things for *another* pack, instead of helping the pack that raised and supported you."

Cindy couldn't formulate an answer fast enough, and Dana kept going.

"You've always been too independent, even from a young age. You didn't want or need our approval to do anything. You decided you were moving out of the pack and had all the arrangements made before you ever even said a word. You sent post cards from Europe before we ever heard you were going to go traveling."

She could have mentioned that she'd stopped asking for advice or permission early on because she'd only received warnings about how her messing up would reflect poorly on the family. It was late, her parents had done as Jonas asked, and they all had a lot to process. She wasn't going to try to fix their relationship standing in the living room right now.

"Why don't you get your bags? We'll make sure the guest room is ready," she said.

They left without another word.

Jonas wrapped his arms around her and held on tight.

"I'm okay. Now, I'm okay. Better, even, because now I can finally just give them up as lost to me. Their opinion of me is no longer relevant to my life. Even if they manage to come back from this, I will never need their approval again. But it was nice to hear what they said, and sort of believe that they meant it."

"I hate that you ever tried to make them proud of you. They're disgusting."

She smiled into his shoulder. "I don't know if having you is helping me let go, or if I was just ready for it, but either way, this hug makes it all easier."

The door opened again, but she wasn't worried. She knew damn well the room was ready for guests. She showed them to it and bid them goodnight. It took her actually biting her lip, but she didn't ask them if they wanted anything to eat or drink before she met Jonas in the hall and walked back to their bedroom.

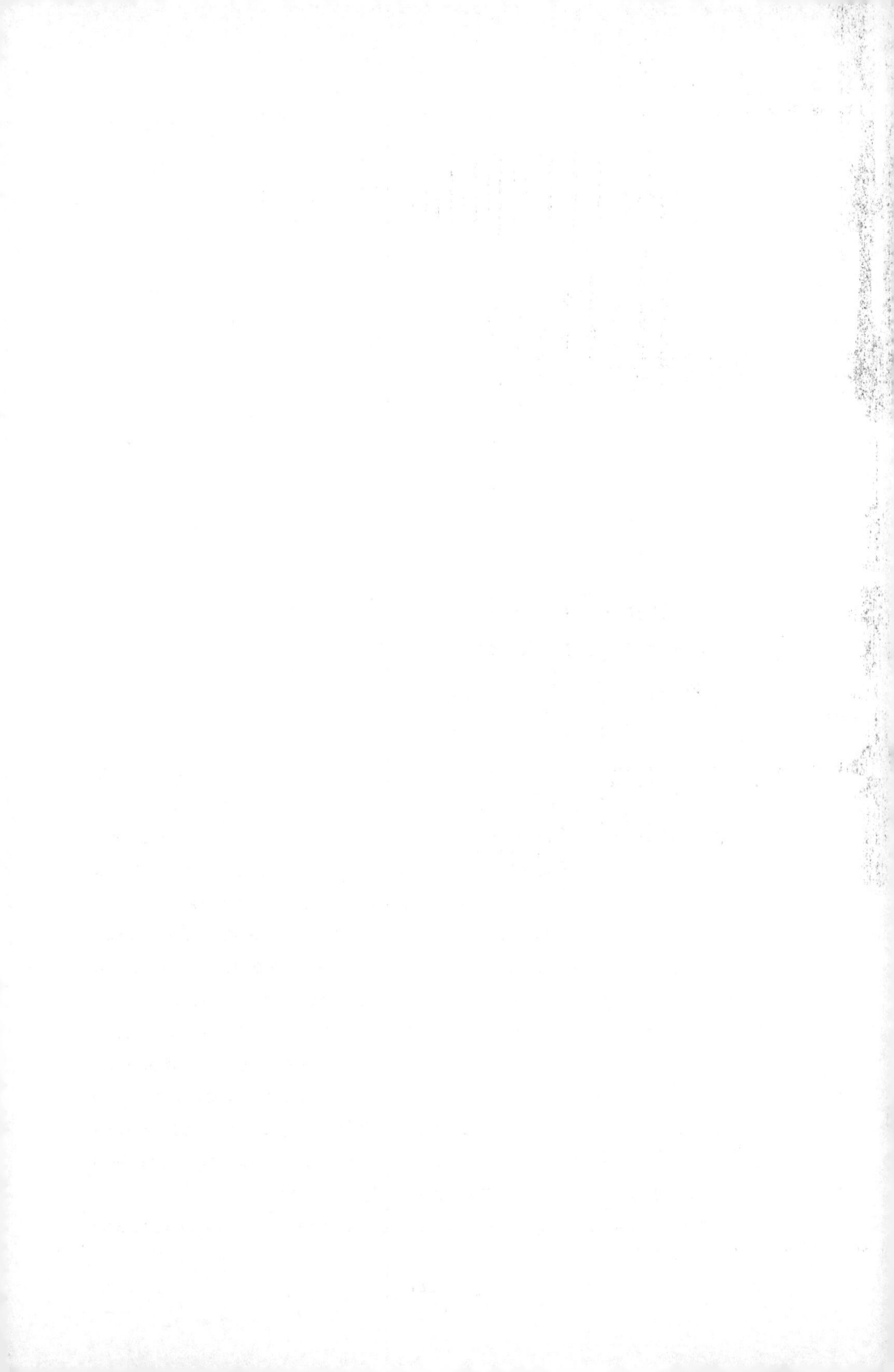

CHAPTER TWELVE

Jonas accepted a beer from Adam with a nod of thanks.

"Your in-laws are dicks," Adam told him, continuing a conversation from earlier.

"Yeah. How they raised that sweet woman, I don't know. And she swears her brother's a good guy."

He and Cindy had seen her parents off early the morning after their ambush, then Cindy had called Myra. Myra and Adam had arrived quickly, and they'd all tried to deconstruct what had happened. Jonas thought it was pretty simple. Brenda had screwed her parents over and they were too stupid to have realized it.

Adam's question of why Brenda would want to join their pack still bothered him, but she wasn't, so he figured it didn't much matter anymore. Cindy considered the issue dealt with, and she and Myra had called the ladies of the pack and suggested a girls-only run. They'd picked a day and time when everyone was available, ditched the guys, gone out to a nice lunch, and then were driving to a new place, so they could explore. She'd texted just before he'd headed to Adam's, to let him know that the exploring part was about to begin and she was turning off her phone.

Jonas was kind of bummed he hadn't been invited. But there was football, and Bill was coming over to join them for the game, so that didn't suck. Cindy had offered to make them some food, but he'd told her to plan a fun girls' day and not worry, they could fend for themselves. He grabbed some frozen pizzas, Adam got the beer, and Bill said he'd bring chips and guacamole. They were set.

"Maybe her brother's a good guy. I trust Cindy's opinion on a lot of things, but her family might be the exception. She certainly never let on how bad her parents were."

"True. I suggested we go up there for a visit soon, and she said as soon as we get the land purchase decided, one way or the other."

"That's good. I know you put your offer in—and we're meeting with your agent tomorrow, by the way, see how we get on with her. Have you heard anything?"

"Yeah, the agent talked to their agent, there was a little back and forth, and we should hear something definitive by Tuesday."

"Nice. I really like that spot, and it's super convenient to the pack house."

"I thought you might," Jonas said, raising his beer to him. "But, tell me the truth. Do you ever miss the hermit life? Cabin deep in the woods, right? I mean, if Myra wasn't a question, if she'd be perfectly happy in that cabin, would you want to be back there, away from the endless drama that comes from a pack? We hardly have any members yet, so you're just getting a tiny sneak peek."

"Trying to scare me off?"

Jonas laughed. "As if you weren't already perfectly aware of what's in store for you. You don't need me to point it out."

"No, I wouldn't go back. What you're really asking is how a guy goes from being a hermit, to having the weight and responsibility of being an alpha."

Jonas nodded. "It's a change."

"You're not wrong. But it's what I needed. What I'm meant to be doing. Denying myself that wasn't helping me any. I was trying to heal, and for a while it's what I needed, but then it just became habit. Almost a crutch."

"Well, in case you haven't figured it out, I'm glad...hell, we're *all* glad that you did come out of the woods and take on the responsibility."

"Aww, shucks," Adam said with a laugh. "But thanks. It's good to hear it. In some ways, it would have been easier to join an established pack. There's a lot of pressure to pick a cohesive group here. I was worried about Olivia and Tasha. Doing right by them. Doing right by the rest of the pack in inviting them. It's worked out better than I thought, faster than I'd thought it would."

"Before they moved in, I was a little hesitant. That first day, still a bit. But Olivia relaxed and warmed up pretty quickly. And now I already can't imagine them not being a part of us." He paused, not sure if it was smart to bring up, but... "I was also worried you might have some animosity for Olivia, since she was with the Mesa pack and didn't do anything to stop the assholes in Phoenix."

Adam nodded. "It was a concern. I was pissed at the whole pack. But when I met her, I just couldn't hold on to it. She makes my wolf protective. I think it was brave of her to ask to come out here, knowing I would be alpha. She assumed we would say no, but she risked being rejected. Did you ask her why?"

"No, I didn't know if it would make her more uncomfortable to ask about the past."

Adam nodded. "Tasha's grandmother, her father's mother, lives in Flagstaff, Arizona. And she's not a werewolf, doesn't know her son became one. Olivia couldn't tell her why they had to move to Chicago. Or why she was able to move south again, but not closer."

Jonas pulled in a deep breath, thinking about Cindy and her layers, nodded his head. "I think we should plan a road trip when school's out."

"I think that would be good," Adam said. "She did try to apologize the other day. I could tell she was scared to bring it up. I didn't let her get very far. I think she's good now."

Bill arrived, and had chocolate chip cookies from Thomas, in addition to the chips and dip, so they were more than set. Neither of the teams playing was any of theirs, so they got to trash talk without any fear of overstepping.

His phone buzzed and he checked the text. "My dad says he's tired of reading recipes, he's coming over. Do we need him to bring anything?"

"Not for now, but maybe he should grab something for dinner. When the ladies get back, they'll be hungry after their run," Adam said.

"Good idea. I'll work that out with him. You guys want to text Thomas and Joe, see if they want to join in?"

They made their plans and returned to yelling at the screen, even though none of them cared about the outcome too much.

His dad arrived in the third quarter with dinner supplies. "Anyone heard from the ladies? Candace isn't much for texting."

"Nope, not yet. Feels like they're having fun out there, though," Adam said.

And he was right. Jonas was getting brief flashes of joy and excitement that made him smile. He was also starting to feel a soft tiredness, so he figured they were winding down their run.

By the time the game ended, Thomas had arrived with wine. Jonas and his dad headed to the kitchen to make the spaghetti while Adam showed Joe, Bill and Thomas the progress they'd made on the guest rooms.

While he chopped the garlic and his dad chopped onion, Jonas filled him in on what had happened with Cindy's parents.

"You bring her over for dinner this week," his dad said forcefully.

Jonas glanced over at him. His expression was fierce and angry.

"You bring her over so she's one hundred percent clear she has parents who love her exactly as she is, even if they're not blood."

"All right, Dad. I will," he said quietly.

His dad nodded and dumped the onions in the skillet, then went rummaging through the spice cabinet to see what was there. He searched out the stockpot and soon they had the meal underway.

The ladies arrived happy and hungry and they all gathered around the large dining room table. It was a lively meal, with Tasha excitedly telling them about the canyon they'd explored, the critters they'd chased and the small but lovely stream they'd rested by.

After dinner and cleanup, they dispersed. His mom joined Olivia, Joe and Bill at the dining room table with Joe's laptop to look at different ideas for decorating the guest rooms with more than the basic beds and sheets Myra and Adam had managed so far. Since it looked like Joe would be running the house eventually, the alpha pair had gleefully handed over the decorating decisions.

Tasha brought out some homework and Jonas' dad nosed his way into seeing what "they were teaching the kids these days," but Tasha seemed to be enjoying explaining her assignment to him.

Myra curled up on the couch next to Adam, and Thomas took the other end. Jen and Jonas took the club chairs, kicking their feet up on the coffee table, with Cindy joining him on his lap. Jen was telling them about the restaurant the ladies had eaten at when Myra's phone rang. She frowned and showed Adam the screen before answering the call.

After only a few seconds, she motioned to Adam and they walked out of the room. Jonas supposed they were going to the library. He raised one eyebrow at Jen, but she just shrugged.

"Jen, how's the job going," Cindy asked.

"Really well. It's such a completely different type of job than it would be in Los Angeles. The nice thing is it gives me time to work with Myra and Adam on how we want security set up here. I went out to the land you guys are taking a look at, and would love to offer some security suggestions if you end up buying it. How's that going, by the way?"

"We should hear something tomorrow or Tuesday," Cindy said.

"And Adam told me he and Myra are giving serious thought to the other parcel. They're going to meet with our realtor. Thomas, we're going to have a lot of questions for you, and work, if you want it. I know you were taking time to settle in and get your own place organized, so just tell us what our boundaries are, and we're happy to work with that."

"I can't resist a good project, so you'll probably have to beat me off with a stick. Did you look at those architectural plan websites I sent you?"

"Yep, and we've narrowed it down to a bunch of styles we like. We definitely have more research to do, though," Cindy told him. "And our realtor is getting information about gas lines, electrical and sewer lines, that kind of thing. I have lists."

"All the fun stuff," Thomas laughed. "And of course you do."

"Exactly. We're really looking—" Cindy cut herself off as Myra and Adam returned.

One look at their faces told Jonas things were serious.

"Can we all gather back at the dining table?" Myra asked. She turned to Tasha as everyone started to comply. "Sweetheart, will you go into the library and work in there for now? This is serious business, and if your mom wants to tell you about it later, or ask you to join us in a while, that's totally up to her. But I need to let her know what it is first so she can make that decision."

Tasha was obviously upset, but she looked to her mom, who gave her a nod. She heaved a sigh, gathered her laptop and notebook, and left the room without a word.

When they'd all taken seats, Myra began. "I wouldn't normally do this in front of a whole pack, but we're so small and so new, I think that everything that happens really does affect all of us, right now."

She looked around the table, receiving nods of agreement from the whole group.

"I've had a call from John Rodriguez," she continued. "He's the alpha in New York, and he used to be in the FBI. Now he works security, but he has a lot of sources there still. He works closely with the National Council, and he has some sort of system in place that triggers him if a werewolf is mentioned in an investigation."

Jen leaned forward, her gaze intent on Myra. Jonas saw Adam put his arm around Olivia's shoulders. She gave him a startled look, but didn't say anything and didn't pull away.

"He said he's found out that someone's reported the truck stop that Olivia is working at as a criminal enterprise. They're looking into it to see if it's worthy of an investigation."

"Whoa," Jen said, sitting back. "If he's had a trigger, then a were-wolf's name was mentioned in the report. Olivia's name."

"That's right," Adam said.

CINDY REALIZED Adam had maneuvered the seating so that Olivia was sitting next to him. She saw the woman's face lose all color. It was so fast, Cindy worried she might faint. Candace must have thought the same, because she was already up and moving towards the kitchen.

Olivia turned to look Adam in the eye. "I swear to you—"

"Olivia," Myra interrupted. "We are absolutely not accusing you of anything. Not one thing. If you did somehow get involved in something, you'll tell us and we'll work it out, but we're starting with the assumption that nobody here has done anything wrong and we're gathering and sharing information."

That stunned Olivia into silence. She accepted the glass of water that Candace put in front of her and took a sip, clearly not sure what was happening.

"I would say it's pretty clear this has something to do with Brenda," Jen said.

Cindy gave Jonas big eyes.

"Wow," Thomas said. "Is it?"

"It is," Myra confirmed. "It would be way too much of a coincidence that the FBI started investigating the truck stop shortly after we upset Brenda. Cindy, is it all right if I share with everyone what you learned from your parents?"

Cindy just nodded, stunned. Jonas wrapped his arm around her shoulders, pulled her in close. She took a deep breath, letting his heat warm her through.

"Okay, please remember that this is all pack business and should not be discussed outside of the pack without serious thought. And it's hearsay at this point. We're not convicting anyone, or even accusing anyone, at least not to any authority…yet. We're just gathering info and updating the pack so we're all aware there's a security concern."

She looked around the table until everyone nodded their understanding again.

"Before we get any further, Olivia, do you think Tasha should be here for this conversation? I didn't want to make that decision for you, but she's nearly an adult, very mature and responsible, so I'm completely on board with including her if you think it's appropriate."

Olivia took in a long breath. "I've done absolutely nothing illegal, and she'll know that, so while it might be upsetting for her, I think it would be best if she were included."

Bill was at the end of the table closest to the door, so he stood up. "I'll ask her to come in."

Olivia looked at Myra. "You believe me."

"Of course we do."

"After the mess with Mesa, it would have been easy for you to assume..." She shook her head. "Others might not have taken the time to think it through."

Myra didn't hesitate in her reply. "We didn't need any time to think it through. You're one of ours. It hasn't been years, but we've all gotten to know each other these last weeks, and yes, I suppose at some point we needed to hear you say it, but there was no doubt in my mind. Our mind," she said, nodding towards Adam.

Olivia didn't have time to respond before Tasha came rushing in. Joe got out of his seat so that Tasha could sit next to her mother.

"Tasha, it will only take a second to bring you up to speed. As you noticed, we didn't talk for very long before your mother decided you were old enough to be included in the conversation. It's going to be a little bit scary, but I want you to know straight off, nothing bad is going to happen. The pack totally has this, we just need to get the details figured out. All right?"

Tasha looked concerned, glanced at her mother, swallowed hard. "All right, Myra, I understand."

"Okay, our friend John Rodriguez, a werewolf who has sources highly placed in the FBI where he used to work, as well as being connected to the National Council, has let us know that there's the possibility of an FBI investigation of the truck stop your mom is working at. We, of course, know your mom is not involved in illegal activities, and, well, we haven't really talked about this part yet, but we think someone is intentionally trying to cause trouble with the pack. Unfortunately, that places your mom at the center of it, but I don't think she's the target specifically. The pack is."

She took a big breath. "The good news is, we found out early and can take steps to shut this down."

"That's…that's not good for Mom," Tasha said, hesitantly.

"It does suck for your mom, but we're going to see that it's fixed. If she loses her job or, more likely it seems to me, the truck stop goes under, we'll be sure she finds something else as soon as possible. We are all in this together. One hundred percent. That part is not in question."

Tasha's eyes filled, but she didn't cry as everyone at the table offered their agreements.

Thomas, on Tasha's other side, put his arm around her, sharing the space with Olivia, giving Tasha extra pack comfort.

Adam cleared his throat, and Cindy was pretty sure his eyes were wet, too. "You're all caught up now, Tasha, except knowing that we suspect Brenda has something to do with this. And we've all already agreed that this is not something we'll be talking about outside of the pack right now. I need you to promise that you'll only talk about this with your mom and us. We want to be very careful before we accuse someone who's innocent, right?"

Tasha frowned, but nodded.

"Right, so that's where we were. What we discovered recently was that Brenda, who is an insurance agent, convinced Cindy's parents to go in on a quote-unquote *investment* and lost them a ton of money. Then she managed to convince them that it was *their* fault they'd lost the money, but she would loan them more money for a different investment that was sure to not only recoup their losses, but set them up for life."

"Seriously?" Bill asked. "People still fall for that load of crap?"

Cindy sighed audibly. "And I swear, they aren't the best parents, but I wouldn't call them dumb."

"To be fair," Jonas added, "she is their fourth. It's normal to have a lot of trust and faith in your hierarchy. And she's been their fourth for a lot of years."

Bill nodded an acknowledgment of that.

"Anyway, when we didn't invite Brenda to join the pack, she went to the McCarthys and basically told them they needed to whip Cindy into shape or she wanted her money back."

"Holy shit," Thomas said. "That's nuts. Do we have any clue why she wants to be here so badly?"

"No clue," Adam said.

"I have some information to add," Jen spoke up.

Myra waved for her to go ahead.

"Before I left tonight, I was going to ask you and Adam if you had time to meet with Olivia and I. She came to me the other day and said she thought there might be something off at the truck stop." She paused until it was quiet again. "She didn't have any proof, and didn't want to accuse anyone without that, but she wanted me to be aware, and to ask my advice on how she might proceed safely. I told her I was going to check at the Sheriff's Office, to find out if there were any old or active investigations, or even rumors about the business, and then we could meet with you guys and fill you in." She nodded to Myra and Adam.

"I found out yesterday that there *is* actually an investigation. The guy in charge of it wasn't in, but he was today. I spoke to him this morning and let him know that I have a friend who just started working there, and he showed me his files. They've suspected a money-laundering operation for some time, but haven't been able to nail anything down."

"Wow," Joe said. "This is like living in a movie." He seemed to think about how that might sound and grimaced at Olivia. "Sorry."

She just shook her head.

"But why would Brenda send one of the pack to apply for a job there if she knew they were corrupt, *and* she wanted to be in our pack?" Cindy asked. "Maybe she doesn't know?"

"Maybe," Adam said. "Although the insurance thing is pretty shady, so..."

Jen shook her head. "No, she had to know, if she's the one who tipped off the feds to try and get Olivia in trouble."

"Oh, right." Adam frowned. "Do we think what she did with Cindy's parents is illegal? Can we get the feds to investigate that?"

"I don't know insurance fraud," Jen said. "But it can't hurt to describe the situation to John and see what he thinks."

Olivia cleared her throat slightly, then spoke, quietly. "I've had some time to think on the things I've found at work. I think I can help the police. I'd like to talk to Jen's colleague."

Myra nodded. "I think that's a good idea. And Jen can tell her coworker that there's a possible federal investigation he might want to check into."

"I'd like to talk to John," Jen said. "Find out if Brenda actually had enough clout to get an investigation started, or if they're really just saying they'll get someone to look into it. Either way, with Olivia being so new, unless she specifically told them that the truck stop hired Olivia to take over the criminal activity, I'm sure they'll consider her at the bottom of their list of suspects. And with my office able to show that Olivia talked to me before Brenda contacted them, I don't think you need to be too worried." She reached over and patted Olivia's hand. "We'll get this sorted."

"Cindy, do you think Brenda has, how did Jen put it? Enough clout to get an actual investigation started?" Candace asked. "It's hard to imagine the FBI would be very interested in a small town truck stop."

Cindy considered. "I think she's pretty good at networking. I can imagine her keeping up certain relationships in case she might be able to use them to her advantage later. I think it's possible she knows someone well enough to push for an investigation, but I also think Jen's right, that Olivia's newness in the position and the fact that she already went to the local police will keep this from getting out of hand."

Adam looked at his watch. "Okay, it's getting late, and Tasha and Joe have school tomorrow."

Joe chuckled.

"We all know what the situation is. Jen and Olivia will meet with the guy investigating from the Sheriff's Office. Myra and I will fill John in. We won't go to Brenda's alpha until we have a little more info. Olivia, if you'd like any one of us to go with you when you meet with…well, anyone, we're here for you."

Everyone around the table nodded.

"Seriously, Olivia," Cindy said. "We want to be there for you. This is a pack issue, you're just the one getting stuck with the shit detail. Please let us be there with you."

She could actually see Olivia's shoulders drop as the woman let go of some of the strain she'd been holding. "I would really like it if you, Adam or Jonas could be with me when Jen and I meet with the deputy."

Cindy smiled. "You got it."

"All right, let's head home for now. Everyone, please try and be a little more aware of your surroundings for a while, just to be on the super-safe side, okay?" Myra asked.

More nods around the table and they all dispersed.

CHAPTER THIRTEEN

Jonas was quiet on their drive home, and Cindy couldn't blame him. She had so many thoughts and questions swirling around in her brain, she didn't know where to start, so she just focused on driving. When they made it inside the house, they collapsed onto the couch.

"Well, that was unexpected," she started.

"Like the bullshit from your parents needed to be topped."

She laughed. "Exactly."

"But I'm really glad that Olivia trusts us to stand with her. Be there for her."

"Me too." She kicked off her shoes, turned so that she was leaning against the arm of the couch, and put her toes under his thigh.

"How do you think this is going to go?" he asked.

She took in a deep breath while she thought about it. "I guess when they get a few facts under their belts, Myra and Adam will talk to Jose, Brenda's alpha. When he questions her, it should all come clear. They just need to have solid reasons to talk to her. And they need as much information as they can gather to know exactly which questions to ask."

Jonas nodded. "I'm glad John is involved. He's a great alpha. He should be able to help Jen navigate keeping the pack and Olivia safe while still letting the police handle their business."

"Will you mind if I'm the one who goes with Olivia to the station?" she asked. "At first I was thinking we should both go, so that she feels plenty of support, but now I'm thinking that might look weird to the deputy."

"Hm, maybe. And no, I don't mind. But I'm happy to go if the timing stinks for you."

She nodded, covered her mouth as she yawned. "It was such a lovely day to end with such craziness."

"I'm glad you guys had a good time."

"We did. It was great getting closer to everyone." She pulled her feet out from under him and stood. He watched her as she pulled her sweater over her head, hooked her thumbs into the top of her skirt and underwear, and pushed them down to her ankles. Stepping free, she straddled him on the couch. His arms immediately came around to hold her, support her.

He didn't say anything, just watched and waited.

She caressed his face with her fingers, from the hairline to his jaw. She held her fingers there, delicately, barely touching—and leaned in to kiss him savagely.

He grunted at the impact, his arms tightening their hold. She speared her fingers into his hair, tugged.

He growled and stood, holding her with one arm while he tried to open his jeans. He cursed into her mouth but she just smiled around the kiss.

When he tore his mouth away, she couldn't help herself. "Problem?"

"I've got it now, you witch," he assured her, then turned and lay her on the couch, pushing into her in one swift thrust.

It felt amazing, like being filled with lightning. She sparked and nearly came, but she needed more of him. He had one knee beside her and the other foot on the floor. She grabbed his thigh and held on while he found his rhythm.

"Touch yourself," he grunted. "I want to see."

She met his gaze and grew even slicker just from his words and from the heat in his eyes. Bringing one hand up to his mouth, she offered him two fingers. He sucked them in hard, bit lightly, laved and tongued them. When she pulled them free, he managed a little kiss.

Without losing eye contact, she moved her wet fingers to her clit, circled and pinched. She clinched her vaginal muscles hard around his cock. Sweat beaded on his forehead and she wanted to lick it off, but he was too far away. He picked up speed, and she lost all rational thought. Only blinding sensations as she worked her clit, watched his eyes, and felt him all the way inside her core.

"I love you, baby," he said.

She lost it, came with his words, her hand stilling, her hips arching.

He thrust again, one more time, and came inside her. She pulled his face down and kissed him softly.

CINDY WOKE up Monday morning with an abundance of energy. Maybe being mated was somehow turning her into a morning person. Or maybe it was the good sex. She grabbed her phone and checked her emails first, in case there was an early message from their realtor, but no. There was, however, a message from her brother, asking when she was going to come visit or offering to come meet Jonas in New Mexico, instead. Either way, he said, it was going to happen soon.

She smiled, but then wondered if her parents had talked to him at all. She pecked out a quick reply that she was definitely bringing Jonas out to meet him and the kids as soon as they sorted some stuff out.

Jonas was still sleeping so she watched for a minute, sighing at how gorgeous he was, and then rolled out of bed.

She smelled coffee when she got out of the shower, and found a mug waiting for her on the counter, perfectly doctored. She tracked him to the kitchen where he was scrambling eggs, wearing sweatpants and no shirt. She bit him on the biceps out of appreciation. Then she kissed him.

The day went up from there, with an email from their realtor saying their offer had been accepted. They made an appointment to put down their deposit and Cindy went back to work, after they celebrated for a little while. Olivia texted to say she was supposed to meet Jen at the Sheriff's Office after she got off work, and did Cindy want to meet her there? Cindy texted back that she would certainly be there, and why didn't she see if Jonas could go over and feed Tasha dinner, so she wouldn't be alone?

Olivia responded with enthusiasm, so she got Jonas on board.

She wasn't at all nervous when she left the house, but by the time she got to the station, she was a little worried that she wouldn't know how best to help Olivia. There wasn't much she could do but go in and see what happened though, so in she went. She gave Olivia a hug in greeting, then followed her to a small office where they were invited to sit.

The deputy who came in with Jen to question Olivia was polite and courteous. He walked her through her first days at the truck stop, and what she'd seen and heard, what had caused her to be suspicious. Cindy kept her mouth shut, and Olivia was straight forward and factual. He seemed excited by the info she had and took a lot of notes. When he was done, Jen gave him John Rodriguez's number and suggested they chat.

Olivia wilted when they walked out of the station and Cindy pulled her into a hug. "You were amazing! I'm so proud of you, and impressed, and you must be exhausted." She looked at her watch. "I think that was the longest two hours of my life."

Pulling herself back up, Olivia nodded. "This may have been the longest *Monday* of my life. All day at work I expected federal agents to burst in. Or drug runners or something."

"I bet. I should have met you at your house so we could take one car and you wouldn't have to drive home."

"Plus, Jonas is at my house so you could have driven home together. I guess we didn't do a very good job of thinking past the meeting. But it went well, and that's what matters. I really, really want to thank you for being there for me."

"You're very welcome, I was happy to lend some support, though you handled it perfectly. Come on, let's get you home and to your girl."

Since she did have her own car, she went straight home and poured two glasses of wine while she waited for Jonas. She'd eaten an early dinner so that she wouldn't be starving during the meeting, but now she was feeling peckish. She grabbed a cutting board and knife, a block of asiago cheese, a handful of crackers, a bunch of grapes, and carefully toted it all to the dining room table.

When Jonas came home, she was cutting slices, so she kept her seat and waited for him to come to her. She lifted her face for a kiss, and he complied before sitting down in front of the second glass of wine and snagging a grape.

"Olivia said it went pretty well," he said.

Cindy nodded. "How was Tasha?"

"Worried, but not terribly so. Relieved when her mom came home tired but in a good mood."

"Excellent. Did you look at house plans today?" she asked

"I did. But there's something else I need to talk to you about first."

She raised her eyebrows at him as she popped a cracker with a slice of cheese into her mouth.

"Your father called me."

She gave him wide eyes and hastily swallowed the food. "You have *got* to be kidding me. What did he say?"

"He said he was sorry their visit hadn't gone well, he and your mother have been under a lot of stress lately, and they let it get to them. He's embarrassed that they lost their savings and they handled it badly."

"To which you asked why he hadn't called me?"

He tipped his glass to her. "Precisely. He said Brenda had told him I wasn't working, but he thought he'd talk to me directly rather than assume the information she'd passed on was legitimate."

"What? What does that even mean?"

"He was calling because he wanted to find out why I wasn't working and how I was planning on supporting you. But he *started* with the apology, probably because he guessed I'd hang up on him if he didn't."

"Hm."

Jonas took a piece of the cheese she'd sliced and ate it with another grape. "I told him it wasn't any of his business, but our financial situation was in order, and that if he wanted any advice or a sounding board on *his* situation, I would be happy to be there for him."

"Hm."

"He said he'd think about that, but he was glad to hear things were okay on my end. He asked if you were home, and I told him you were helping out a packmate and tomorrow might be better to try and reach you."

"Hm."

He leaned in and kissed her, his eyes twinkling. "You're adorable."

"Hm." He laughed, and she had to join him. "Yeah, well, you're gone on me, so it's easy for you to think so." She paused. "Do you think my dad was working his way towards asking you, or me, for money?" she asked.

"I don't know. I don't think so, but maybe. What will you do if he asks?"

She sighed. "I don't know."

"You don't owe them help. Especially financial."

"Would you be upset if I decided to anyway?"

"No."

"That easy? We don't even know how much they're in for."

"That easy. Once we have all the facts, I might offer an opinion on whether I think it's smart or not, but whatever you decide, I'll back you. Doesn't matter if it's a logical or emotional decision."

"You're freaking awesome." She leaned over and rested her head on his shoulder.

"You're tired."

She sighed. "Yeah. I was a bit stressed about the meeting, and stress tires me out."

"I can probably find a way to de-stress you," he murmured.

She laughed. "I'm not stressed anymore, just tired. It's an aftereffect."

"Let's put on a silly movie and you can fall asleep on top of me on the couch. Then I can wake you early in the morning and sex you up all kinds of ways without feeling guilty about depriving you of your sleep."

"All kinds of ways?" she asked.

"All kinds."

"Deal."

CHAPTER FOURTEEN

"It's over," Cindy told Jonas on the phone several days later.

"What?" He put down his hammer and walked away from the shed he and Thomas were building.

"The Sheriff's Department raided the truck stop. Olivia's okay, she called me. And she said Jen told her that Brenda's getting charged, too. Though she didn't have specifics."

"Wow."

"Yeah. Myra didn't answer her phone, shockingly enough."

"Was Olivia heading home?" he asked. "I can go over there, see if she needs something."

"She was going to, but I suggested she grab Tasha and we meet up at the pack house. See if anyone else wants to meet up. It helps that it's Friday. We can have a, what do you call it, like an after-action report or whatever. And then we can gossip. We can get pizzas. I texted Myra to see if she's good with that, I'll let you know as soon as she answers."

"A debriefing, I think. And that sounds good to me."

She laughed. "Remembering that word would have made the text to Myra easier."

He went back to the shed and updated Thomas, who called Bill out of the trailer to give him the news as well. It wasn't long before he had a text confirming the pack house debriefing was on. Cindy said she and Olivia were handling contacting everyone and organizing food, so he was able to go back to the construction efforts. By the time they were ready to clean up and head to the house, the shed was complete. Bill came back out to offer his compliments. Thomas said it was Bill's job to paint it, and they started a *discussion* about the color.

Laughing as he told them goodbye, Jonas went home to shower.

When they arrived at the house, everyone was there except Jen, who didn't get off work for another hour.

They gathered in the kitchen as Cindy and Olivia handed out plates and drinks. There were pizza boxes on the counter and a thick stack of napkins. He kissed his mate and grabbed a slice of sausage and mushroom and one of buffalo chicken.

"Jen said she's eating at work, that's why we're not waiting," Adam said as they all found seats at the table.

"How did the shed building go," Myra asked before taking a bite of her slice.

"It certainly looks great," Bill offered. "It will look even better when I've painted it barn red."

Thomas growled. "It's not a barn, you can't paint it red."

"There's no rule that says barn red is only allowed on barns."

"It's in the name!"

Everyone burst out laughing, and Thomas picked an olive off his pizza and threw it at his mate.

"How was school, Tasha? Anything fun and exciting today?" Adam asked.

"No, but Mom did tell me that you said the Changs decided they're going to move here. I'm super excited about that. Can you give them my cell phone number so Blaire can text me? I'm bummed they're not coming until summer, but at least we'll be able to have fun before school starts."

"Absolutely," he promised.

"When does Latisha get here," Joe asked. "Next month, right?"

"That's her plan right now," Myra confirmed. "Adam and Jonas volunteered to drive out to meet her. One of them will drive her moving truck back. She's going to fly."

"Awesome," Tasha said, her mouth full.

Olivia gave her a look that had Tasha flushing.

"If you guys want company, let me know," Robert said. "I wouldn't mind that road trip."

"Any word from Becky and Soo?" Candace asked.

Myra nodded. "They're really hoping to make it work, just worried about the job situation. I told them there was no rush, the invitation was open, it doesn't have an expiration date."

They ate pizza and chatted about everything except the situation at hand. Jen arrived shortly after they'd cleaned up and they regathered at the table.

"Okay. Here's what we know," Adam said. "Federal agents worked with our deputy, and showed up at the truck stop late this afternoon. They took the files and computers and sent everyone home, telling them not to come back."

"So none of the working employees were held?" Joe asked.

"No, they didn't seem interested in anyone who was at work," Olivia answered. "As the manager, I'm the one they gave the warrant to. They asked me to call everyone into the diner, checked people's names off of a list as they identified themselves, and then told us all we could go."

Robert was sitting next to her, and he patted her arm. "That must have been distressing."

"It probably was for the other employees," Olivia said. "For me, it was a relief, because it was awkward knowing something was wrong, something like this was going to be happening, but needing to act like everything was normal."

"Yeah, that had to have sucked," Bill said.

Olivia just nodded. "Of course, now I don't have a job, but that seems crass to think about after all that's happened."

"Not at all," Myra assured her. "We will definitely work on that. As for the rest of this nastiness...I spoke to Jose, Brenda's alpha. I had filled him in a few days ago, with what we knew and what was happening as far as the investigations. When I called to let him know of today's events, he said he was ready to bring Brenda in. Then he called back to let me know she had confessed to skimming money from her clients for years, getting into deep financial trouble herself and screwing Cindy's parents and another client—not a pack member—in order to get herself out of it. She'd hoped by leaving town and coming to a tiny pack, that she'd escape discovery."

"What does our being a small pack have to do with anything?" Candace asked.

"Hierarchy, I would bet," Adam answered. "She figured she'd be higher up here than fourth."

There was a lot of overlapping reaction, but Jonas tuned it out and studied Cindy. She was shaking her head slowly.

"I can't believe she thought she'd get away with all that," she said.

"She did for a number of years," he pointed out.

"So," Tasha began, hesitatingly. "Her alpha asked her questions and she had to answer him with the truth, right?"

"Right," Adam said.

"And she got away with it all these years because no one suspected anything was wrong, therefore no one asked any questions."

"Right again," Adam said.

"Wow," she said.

"He confirmed that she doesn't have any money, unfortunately," Myra continued. "Her house is mortgaged to the hilt. So there's not much chance of getting anything back for those she swindled."

"How long have you been waiting to work the word swindled into the conversation?" Cindy asked.

They all chuckled.

"You know me too well," Myra said with a grin. "I'm sorry about your parents. I can't think of any way to help, but if anyone has ideas about that, let me know." She looked around the table. "Have I missed anything? Jen?"

"I can confirm that neither the Sheriff's Office or the feds are interested in Olivia as anything other than a witness, and they're pretty thankful for what she was able to give them. It sped things up on their end. That, and apparently they received an anonymous data file that corroborated what Olivia had told them, as well as some stuff she didn't have access to. That's why they were able to move forward."

Olivia blushed as the others offered congratulations.

"Have we figured out why Brenda wanted to get someone hired there?" Bill asked.

"Oh, yes, Jose did question her about that. She just wanted to have done a favor for the pack. She was certain that would make an already obvious invitation a slam dunk."

"Kind of delusional, isn't she?" Joe asked.

"Kind of," Adam agreed. "Apparently she had used them to launder money in the past. So she knew what they were up to, but they've been at it a long time, so she had no reason to think they'd get found out. When we didn't extend an invitation to join the pack, she was so pissed, she contacted someone she knew at the treasury department, not caring that her old friends would get destroyed by the trouble she was trying to cause Olivia and the pack."

"Wow," Tasha said again.

"Of course, there was already a local investigation happening, but she didn't know that."

His dad was shaking his head. "This is all just crazy. I thought New York was lively, but it was nothing like here."

His mom slapped his shoulder but everyone else laughed.

Myra's phone beeped and she checked the display. "That's John," she said, reading the message. "They've arrested the owners of the truck stop. One guy got shot, but otherwise smooth operation."

"Oh, well then," Cindy said. "Smooth."

"Who's up for a run," Adam asked. "I think we've gotten all we're going to get from this tonight."

"Excellent idea," Myra said, kissing her mate.

They raced into the night, yipping and playing for several hours.

They rested before meandering back and making their way into the house, where they piled on the living room rug and slept as a pack.

Jonas woke early and nudged Cindy awake. She yawned and pulled herself free of the wolf pile, and they went into the laundry room to change and put on their clothes. Cindy was still sleepy and she leaned into him, soft and warm. He breathed in deep, loving the scent of wolf and mate and woman, all Cindy.

"We could stay here for breakfast, or I can make you pancakes and keep you naked all day at home," he said.

"Mmm, pancakes and naked Jonas. I don't even have to think about it."

They quietly let themselves out of the house and he drove them home. She'd gotten a ride with Myra, so they didn't have to worry about a second car.

He made them pancakes and she juiced oranges and heated maple syrup. Which gave him interesting ideas. She saw him eyeing the bottle, and the twinkle in her eye and the shit-eating grin told him she was on the same page.

They ate a lot of pancakes and decided they weren't feeling quite that sexy with full stomachs, so they took his laptop to the bed and checked out different houses and blueprints. Naked.

"These three," Cindy said. "Definitely one of these three."

Jonas nodded. Then pointed. "That's the one." He'd noticed how many times she'd come back to this particular plan, and he liked it a lot.

She nodded. "Yeah, that one." She said it softly and turned to him for a kiss.

He moved the laptop to the bedside table, then slid down, pulling her on top of him as he did so. She rested her arms across his chest, dropped her chin to her arms and stared at him.

"I think we're doing pretty well with this whole mate thing, don't you?" she asked.

"I think we're doing very well with it."

"I wonder if Brenda would have turned out differently if she'd met her mate. I wonder if she still will."

He wrinkled his nose. "Seems like she started taking advantage of people pretty early."

"Yeah."

"Did your dad call you?" he asked. He figured she'd have told him if they'd spoken, but it had been several days, so he asked.

"He tried, but I didn't answer. I texted him and said you'd told me about the chat you guys had, and I was thinking about things, but I wasn't ready to talk to him or Mom yet."

"Fair enough. Did he answer back?"

"He said he would be there when I was ready."

"That's a fairly good sign."

"Yes."

"Let's go visit your brother. You don't have to see your parents, you can decide when we're there if you feel like it. I'd like to meet him and his family."

"Okay."

"That's it?" He ran a finger up and down her back, lightly, not starting anything, just feeling her.

"Yep. I want to visit, too. I want you to meet them. I think it's time, now that the pack's settled down a little. Although I wish we could do something to help Olivia find a job. I thought about trying to fit her in with the blog, but I've got everything handled with people I love, so there's really no room for her."

"I was thinking that Mom and Dad could buy the truck stop, and she could stay on as manager. They could have fun with that, I think."

She gasped. "That would be amazing! Do you think they will?"

"I don't know how it works, with the investigation. If the business can be sold or what. But it would be pretty cool, because it would be a source for other jobs. Olivia mentioned to me that once she got her feet under her as manager, she was going to make some suggestions about increasing business, which would allow for more employees."

"A good spot for future pack members."

"If my parents do like the idea of the truck stop, I'll help them with it. It's a bigger venture than what I first suggested to them. It might be cool to help set up different businesses, get them going. First the truck stop, then a pub or café or whatever. Then something else. Maybe involving other pack members with each venture."

"And all businesses that offer employment to pack members, so we can keep growing, which in turn grows the businesses."

"Exactly. But to start, I don't know about the investigation," he reminded her.

"Still, it will be cool to see what your parents think."

"I didn't want to bring it up last night, in front of everyone, but I'll go by their place later today."

"Awesome. Maybe I'll come with you. If I decide to let you out of bed."

CINDY GRINNED AT JONAS. She decided the pancakes had settled quite well by now. She'd had a wonderful run with the pack, a fantastic breakfast, had picked out the plans for her future home with the man she loved, and now she was ready to rock his world.

She sat up, her knees on either side of his hips. His hands fell naturally to her thighs as he waited to see what she wanted to do. One of the things she loved about him was his equal willingness to sit back and let her lead, or to take charge and leave her utterly breathless.

Rising up to her knees, she tried to bring forth her internal sex kitten. Or porn star. Or something. She pushed her fingers into her hair, holding her elbows out, keeping her gaze steady with his.

He licked his lips.

She bit hers.

He growled.

She ran her hands down her neck and cupped her breasts, plumping them and pushing them together. His hands traveled from her thighs to her hips, and he gripped tight, like he needed something to hold on to. She plucked one nipple, then the other, but they were already hard points. She squeezed tight and couldn't hold back a gasp.

His chest heaved as he drew in a sharp breath.

She let one hand drift down, teased through her curls, then slowly slid one finger deep inside. His groan sounded pained, but he didn't move. A smiled stretched across her face. His answering grin made her feel bold.

"Let me taste," he growled.

She trailed the wet finger up his chest to his lips. He sucked it in, tonguing it clean. She pulled free and used the finger to circle and tease his nipples.

"How long are you planning on torturing me?" he asked.

"Four minutes," she said, pulling the number out of nowhere.

He immediately checked his watch and she had to bite her cheek not to laugh.

His hand went back to her hip.

She supposed she should check the time, too, but figured he'd keep her on track. She braced one hand on his abs and pulled the other back between her legs. Sliding two fingers in this time, getting them nice and wet before she moved them to her clit. She shut her eyes, tilted her head back and sighed. Her hips started to move, her toes curling.

"You are so beautiful," he whispered. "So strong and smart and sexy as all fuck."

This time her smile was soft, but she didn't look at him. She could feel him watching her, without needing to see. Sensations bloomed inside of her as she felt him, as she teased herself, as she imagined what he was seeing.

"I want you inside me," she said, not remembering how much time was left. Not caring. She opened her eyes and looked back down at him.

"I want to taste you first," he said.

"Well, if that's really what you want," she teased.

She dropped down beside him, plumped the pillow under her head and grinned. "You may begin."

"You are so good to me," he said, taking his pillow and putting it under her hips. He kneeled over her, leaned down to kiss her. His tongue tangled with hers and they banged teeth. She laughed, but had to stop so she could breathe without breaking the kiss. He finally lifted up with a gasp. The heat in his eyes had her already-tingling body nearly combusting.

"Well, get to it then," she said.

"Mmm."

He kissed her collarbone, tasting the hollow of her neck, then teased little kisses around her breasts. She speared her fingers into his hair and tried to direct him to her nipple, but he just smiled against her chest and kept at it. So she let go of his head and pinched her own nipple. He huffed out a laugh and pulled her other nipple between his lips, hard.

She lost her concentration and just held her breast while he worked one, then the other, biting her fingers when he decided they were in the way. He gave one last kiss to the area between her breasts and kissed a slow path down to her belly button.

"Put your tongue in there and you will lose a handful of hair," she said.

He snorted. "Did you really think I'd forgotten your previous warnings?"

"It pays to be proactive," she said with a sniff.

"Mmm-hmm." He brushed over the sensitive spot with his nose, but that was it. And then his whole body stilled.

One second. Two.

Finally, he looked up at her—and her breath caught at the expression on his face. Amazement and happiness and so much love.

"What," she asked, holding her breath.

"You're pregnant."

Her jaw dropped open. "*What?*"

"I can smell the life inside of you."

"Oh my god. A baby. Our baby!"

"Our baby." He rose back up and kissed her, a totally different kiss then before. Soft and gentle and sweet.

Which was awesome. For a minute. But her body was still pulsing with need for him. She grabbed his head between her hands and sucked his tongue in, hard. He got the hint. Which was good because she was no longer interested in waiting. She wrapped her legs around his hips and dug her feet into his butt.

"Inside me. Get inside me," she demanded.

He reached a hand between them, guided himself to her core, and pushed hard and fast and deep and perfect. She brought her hips up to meet him as he withdrew and thrust again, matching his rhythm, feeling their connection, body, heart and soul.

"Mine," he said. "All mine."

"So very mine," she agreed. It came out in three gasps as he worked her, wound her up and up until she could do nothing but soar. She cried out, a long, thin wail that almost masked the sound of his release.

He dropped down to her side, draped one leg and one arm over her, and rested his head on her shoulder.

"Damn," she said when she could speak again.

"You have such a way with words."

"It's a gift."

He looked up at her. "Should I be schmaltzy now and tell you that you're a gift?"

"If you feel like it. But as long as you keep doing what you just did for many, many years to come, I already know you think it."

"Doesn't mean it shouldn't be said," he pointed out.

"True enough."

He kissed her. "You're the best gift I've ever had, better than I ever imagined you would be."

"I love you. I can barely remember what it's like not to have you in my life. I'm so thankful for you."

"Well, I am pretty awesome. At least that's what my parents tell me."

"Agreed."

He put his head back down on her shoulder.

"A baby," he whispered.

"Our baby," she whispered.

"Good thing we picked a four-bedroom house plan."

CHAPTER FIFTEEN

Cindy snatched up her squealing niece as the toddler hurdled forwards, arms stretched wide. "Hello, my lovely Sara! I've missed you." Danny, her older-by-eighteen-months nephew, bounced around, waiting for his turn. She dropped down to her knees and pulled him in to join the hug.

She heard Jonas introducing himself to Bill and Juanita. She kissed both faces several times, then stood back. "Guys, do you want to meet my mate, Jonas?" Danny nodded solemnly and Sara ducked her head.

Jonas knelt down next to her. "Hi," he said. "You must be Danny." He held out a hand and Danny shook it enthusiastically.

"And you must be Sara." He held his hand out, but Sara leaned in and kissed his cheek, then buried her face in Cindy's chest. Cindy picked her up and stood, finally turning to her brother and his mate.

"Hey, kid," Bill said, wrapping his arms around her. "I'm happy for you."

"Just for me?" she asked with a grin.

"Both of you," he assured her.

"How about all three of us?" she asked.

His eyes went wide, and then he hugged her again, causing Sara to shriek in laughter from between them.

"Congratulations," Juanita told her when she finally managed to get her own hug. "That's fantastic news."

"We haven't told anyone yet, it's very early days, so keep it to yourselves for now."

They went into the lovely adobe house. Bill had offered to pick them up from the airport, but Cindy had insisted it was easier for them to rent a car. She had agreed that they'd stay a couple of nights, though, so Jonas carried their bag in as well.

Sara ran off to get her doll to show them and Danny countered with his teddy bear. They took turns with Cindy and Jonas, bringing in different toys until there was a small pile on the table and Sara was falling asleep in Jonas' arms, having long abandoned her initial shyness.

Bill took the kids in for a nap and Juanita brought snacks to the table.

"All right," Bill said when he returned. "Tell me what's going on with Mom and Dad."

She wrinkled her nose. "I think you should talk to them about that."

"I'm talking to you."

"If they wanted you to know, they'd tell you." She paused. "Why, what do you know?"

"You guys are third of your pack," Jonas interrupted. "And according to our alpha, *your* alpha knows everything. Seems like he'd share that, especially with the son and daughter-in-law of the two people most affected."

Cindy scowled at her brother. "Yeah."

Bill's lips twitched at that, but he didn't laugh so she didn't have to hit him. "I wasn't sure you were in on all of it, and I didn't want to pass along privileged information just because you're my sister."

Cindy rolled her eyes. She couldn't exactly disagree, but still. Since she believed him, she gave a quick summary.

"Has Mom or Dad said anything to you about the money?" she asked.

"No. I thought about going to talk to them, but wanted to wait since you were coming, see what you think."

"Now that we know what we know," Juanita said, "it's easy to see that they were anxious and upset the last few years. But they never opened up to us."

Cindy scoffed. "Well, if they didn't open up to you guys, we know they weren't going to talk to me about it. At least they weren't until the Brenda thing happened and they felt they had a reason to yell at me and that would help them."

Bill shook his head. "They were under a lot of stress, otherwise I can't imagine them thinking that was okay to do."

Her gut clenched at the memory. She felt she'd come a long way in not needing their validation and support, but that didn't mean the lack of it didn't suck.

Juanita sighed. "I've never understood how two people can be such good parents to Bill and our family and such lousy parents to you."

"They treat you like a typical black sheep, but you don't have any of the benefits of being a black sheep," Bill agreed.

She laughed. "I'm the most boring black sheep out there. I never dyed my hair, I never blasted heavy metal, and I went off to support myself with a good career. I suck at being a black sheep."

Jonas took her hand, knowing that just because she could joke about it, didn't mean it didn't hurt.

"After Sara was born, Dad and I were having dinner together, just the two of us. I don't remember where everyone else was. Anyway, he'd had a couple of beers, and was sipping on a whiskey so he was a little more talkative than normal. He said that he and Mom had always known they'd have a son, and that he'd be powerful." He made rabbit ears with his fingers on the last word. "And they were totally surprised when you came along. It's like they never quite believed they were supposed to have a second child."

"That sort of makes sense," she agreed.

"It's awful," Jonas said.

"They weren't terrible to me," she pointed out. "They just weren't great. Or even particularly good."

"Which was made worse by the fact that they were great with me," Bill added.

"Yeah."

"I hated that you left, but I was proud of you for doing it, and for doing it so well," Bill said.

"Aww, I know it. You were good about letting me know. And making me the cool auntie, letting me have that even though I don't see the kids that often."

"They love the shit out of you," he said.

She took a deep breath, reminding herself that she had so many amazing people in her world, she didn't particularly need those two who'd given her life.

"Anyway, I might go talk to them, but I'm not feeling particularly inclined to bail them out."

"You better not," Bill growled. "They have not earned that from you. They still work, they can still save for retirement. We'll see how things are when it gets closer to that scenario."

She just raised her eyebrows at him but didn't argue.

"How is your pack doing? It must be hard having a member of your hierarchy fail her people so badly."

"It's been tough," Juanita said. "People are confused and hurt. The loss of trust is really hard. We've had pack members here to dinner most every night so they can talk and vent and get reassurance. They need to spend time with us, confirm their trust in us."

"To be honest, that's what gave me the strength to leave all those years ago. Not trusting Brenda, and not trusting that I could share those feelings with Mom and Dad. That's when I realized staying here was sort of pointless. But I am sorry that I didn't speak up about Brenda."

"Oh no, don't take that on yourself. You didn't have enough information, you were just out of college, and besides, she wasn't doing enough for anyone to really call her on it." Her brother gave her his best stern expression.

"No, but it might have been enough to question her, keep an eye on her." She shook her head. "I don't know."

"Bill's right, none of that is on you, and nobody thinks otherwise," Juanita said.

A weight she hadn't realized she'd been holding on to lifted. "Okay."

"Here's an idea. You tell me if you're comfortable with it," Juanita said. "We take you guys out to a nice dinner, celebrate your finding each other and the pregnancy. We ask our usual babysitters, your mom and dad, to come over while we're out. When we get back from dinner, if you feel up to sitting with them, we can do that. Together. And if you don't, Bill and I see them off with thanks, as usual."

She thought about it. Thought about telling her parents that she and Jonas were having their grandchild, giving them a chance to be better. Was it worth it, to open herself up to that? Maybe.

"Okay. That's a good plan."

They went to a wonderful mom-and-pop restaurant with terrible lighting, rustic tables and fantastic steaks. She enjoyed watching her mate get to know her brother and sister-in-law. Jonas was clearly pleased to see that Bill and Juanita were good to her, after the fiasco of meeting her parents.

When they got back to the house, they gathered in the living room. Bill told their parents about the meal, small talk to make things easier. When he was finished, her dad turned to her.

"Cindy, I want—we want—to apologize, for before. We let the situation get out of hand, we were stressed. It's not an excuse. We should never have treated you that way, and we're sorry."

Her mom took his hand. "You've been a good daughter. Always. We haven't told you that." She looked at Jonas. "You made us look in the mirror, see what we'd done. Or hadn't done. Thank you for that. And thank you for being there for Cindy."

Cindy's throat tightened. She'd told herself she didn't need their validation, and she didn't, but it was really, really nice to have it. She took a deep breath. "Thanks. I appreciate that."

Her father looked like he was going to launch into more, but she held up a hand. "Let's leave it at that for now. It's late and the kids will be up early."

They looked disappointed, but didn't argue, just said their goodbyes.

Cindy hugged Bill and Juanita and took Jonas' hand. They went into the guest bedroom and he wrapped his arms around her and held her tight while they listened to the other two close up the house, turn off the lights, check on the kids. When they heard the bedroom door close, she lifted her face out of his sweater.

"I don't know why I'm crying," she whispered.

"It was a lot. You're allowed to feel that."

"Let's go sit on the porch." She felt like a teenager sneaking out of the house as they tiptoed through the dark rooms to the front door. It had begun to rain on their drive back from dinner, but the porch was covered. He grabbed a blanket that was on the back of the living room sofa and wrapped them up in it before sitting them on a chair that wasn't meant to hold two. But he made it work.

"I want one of those porch swings. With a bunch of pillows," she told him.

"Bright colors," he guessed.

"Of course."

"It should only be a couple more days and the land is officially ours."

"I'm so happy," she said.

"Me, too."

The rain fell all around them, but they were snug in the little cocoon. They'd be able to do this at home, she thought. Watch the rain or the stars. Sit together after a long day, when their own child was asleep inside.

"We have to start thinking of names," he said. "Start a list."

"Yeah. And tell your parents. They'll be so freaking excited. We should think of a fun way to tell them. World's Best Grandparent shirts, or something like that."

His arms tightened around her, and she knew she was home. Didn't matter that she was at her brother's house, in a different state. Didn't matter that the beautiful house they wanted to build didn't exist yet. She was wrapped up in his arms, so she was home.

EXCERPT

Wolf Called
By KB Alan
(Available now for pre-order
Release date: 1/27/2023)

Blurb:

When Ivy runs into the hard-bodied hottie with the gorgeous eyes and sexy forearms, she's kind of in the middle of breaking the law. Technically. Maybe. And he's almost certainly a cop. Or military? Hard to say, but he's cagey and he makes her lady parts tingle so there's only one thing to do. *Run.*

Mountain Pack security specialist Brad isn't sure what's happening with the human woman who catches his eye and then runs away. But he's fairly certain she's guilty of something. And he's almost as certain she's his mate. Maybe. What's absolutely clear is that he's going to find out. He just has to catch her first. And as a werewolf, that'll be the easy part. Figuring out what to do with her when he finds her, that might be more difficult. But he's absolutely up for the challenge.

Excerpt:

Chapter One

Ivy glanced at her watch. She wasn't concerned about the time, not really. She'd mostly needed an excuse to tear her attention away from the sexy guy working on the office building two doors down. Her table at the cafe had given her a perfect view of the man as he'd circled the building with someone she presumed was the owner or manager, taking notes on a tablet as the other man talked and gestured. She was betting on owner. He was more distraught than she'd imagine a manager would be, as he pointed out the broken windows and spray paint.

She wasn't sure what her hottie's role in this was. Insurance adjuster? Police officer? He'd rolled up in a black SUV just as she, her brother Ty, and his best friend Eddie had taken their seats. His scan of the area as he'd stepped out and made his way to the office had taken her in. Taken all of them in. But she'd felt like he'd paused just a little bit longer on her. Or maybe she was justifying to herself the casual staring she'd been doing since he'd come back outside to do the tour of the damages.

Their waiter had noticed her interest, though misinterpreting it, and told them there'd been a rash of petty vandalism in the area. Likely kids on summer break, the young man—who was almost certainly a kid on summer break—had said, before heading off to place their orders. They'd eaten their late breakfast and Ty and Eddie had decided to go check out the little hardware store, while she lingered over coffee. They had a six-hour drive to get back to their home just outside of Portland.

The guys had joined her on the road trip when they'd learned a comedian they liked was doing a show at the casino nearby. Since her trip was work related and her gas would be covered whether they came along or not, the guys only had to split the cost of a room and some food, so they'd jumped at the chance to join her. Of course, they'd tried to make it seem like they were doing her a favor, saving her from having to make the road trip on her own. She'd just rolled her eyes at that foolishness. Twelve hours on her own, to listen to an audio book while driving through the Pacific Northwest, would have been a treat. But she'd enjoyed giving them this chance. They were home for summer, but would be going back to college soon, and she'd miss Ty.

The owner seemed to run out of steam, hands on his hips, head bowed. The other guy—she would *not* think of him as *her* guy—put a reassuring hand on his shoulder, and gestured with his tablet to the front door. They headed to the door and Ivy figured it was probably time to retrieve the boys and hit the road.

As he held the door open for the business owner, the man she'd been watching lifted his head and stared directly at her.

She felt it. How could you feel a look? She didn't know, but the weird flutter in her stomach told her she wasn't imagining it. And it wasn't the flutter of nerves, of caution. It could have been. Maybe even should have been. She was a Black woman at a small cafe in middle-of-nowhere Idaho, being watched by a white man. But her flutter didn't feel like a warning.

A small grin widened his lips. Shit, was that a dimple? No, she was too far away to see a dimple, surely. He dipped his chin, giving her a small nod, then headed inside.

She resumed breathing. Son of a bitch, apparently when she decided to wake up, she *woke the hell up.*

Her last relationship had ended just over a year ago, and it had ended hard. She'd been closed up ever since. Six months ago, she'd bought a vibrator. Last month, it had shorted out and she'd started thinking it was time to open back up, introduce something a little warmer than silicone back into her life. Nothing serious, she had no interest in that. But a little fun, as long as communication was open and both parties were fully aware that she wasn't in the market for serious.

Giving her whole body a little shake, she sent her brother a text to meet her at the car, and laid cash on the tray the waiter had brought. She took the receipt and used a pen from her purse to circle the items that had been hers and tucked it into her wallet so she could add it to her business expenses. Thinking on that, she took a slow glance around the area. She'd been too busy watching the proceedings next door to give it a proper look earlier. Could she live out here? If she got the offer?

This little town only had a few businesses. A couple of food places, a bar, post office, gas station. Some offices, like the title company with the vandalism trouble. A mom-and-pop market. But there was a real city about forty minutes away. Smaller than her own, but big enough to have real restaurants, hotels, movie theaters and the like. The nearby casino, too. And besides, she wouldn't need to move out here permanently.

The idea was that she'd work closely with Arturo, who owned a small wealth management company, for six months, and slowly transition most of his clients over so he could retire. She'd been a certified financial planner on his team for three years now, along with two others filling the same role, so she already had clients of her own, had some dealings with his. But he'd picked her, potentially, to slide into the top slot when he was ready to move on, and they'd agreed that though most of the business was done either virtually or when they traveled to their clients a few times a year, for this big of a transition, it would be best if they were in the same office for a while.

She'd come out here to meet with him, interview for the promotion, make sure they were on the same page about how the business should be run, and what the future of the company looked like. And to make sure she'd be comfortable moving out to the remote area. She was pretty confident she'd nailed the interview. She and Arturo had always gotten on well together, and he'd recognized that she had more ambition than just being part of the team. As he'd acknowledged in their discussion, he knew if he didn't pick her, he wouldn't get to keep her at the firm for much longer, as she'd move on to bigger things for herself. But she hoped he'd pick her. She didn't actually want bigger, she just wanted more.

This place was not bigger, that was for sure, but her role in the company could be. *Would be*, she decided. She'd aced the interview, damn it, and would be running Mountain View Wealth Management inside of a year. And living here, to get there, wouldn't be a hardship. She was surrounded by farmland and forests, and the weather these last few days of June had been quite a bit warmer than she was used to in Oregon, but that didn't suck. She scratched absently on her arm. She'd need to stock up on lotion, it was hella dry out here.

Feeling lighthearted that her decision was made and she only needed Arturo to make the offer, she headed to her car. Deciding she wanted the lip balm out of her makeup bag, she aimed for the trunk, where she'd put her small suitcase. She'd let the guys sleep in after their late-night show. They'd checked out of the motel just before the ten o'clock deadline, then headed here for breakfast. Even with their long drive, they'd be home before Nana Stevens' Sunday dinner.

"Ivy!"

The shout had her turning towards her brother and Eddie as they jogged across the street. She narrowed her eyes as they paused to let a car pass by. Would it really have been so hard for them to walk the half block to the corner, like she had? She reminded herself that this was a small town with very little traffic, and likely no one cared. The fact that there wasn't even a stop sign for the crosswalk meant she was probably worried for nothing. But really, the corner was *right* there.

She frowned, looking into the trunk, her nose wrinkling at the sour odor. *What the hell was that?* Reaching in, she pulled Eddie's backpack toward her so she could check behind it, not seeing her bag.

"Ivy!" Her brother was panting as he jogged up. "We moved your bag to the backseat." He put his hand on the trunk and started to close it.

"Hey!" She jerked her hand back, still holding the pack. A sharp crack sounded as the lid hit the bag. She jerked it free and shot a glare at her brother, but only had a half second to wonder what his problem was when the smell hit her. What had been a subtle stink when she first opened the trunk was now an eye-watering reek that actually had her stomach churning.

"Holy shit, what the fuck?" she asked, dropping the bag and moving back.

Ty gagged, and he and Eddie both backpedaled away from the trunk.

"Ivy!" Ty shouted for the third time. "Damn it!"

She felt the wrath of the ancestors move through her as she fought the urge to dry heave. Backing up farther, she rounded on her brother. "Tyson Steven Carter, *what did you do?*"

He blinked at her, then looked around them to see who was listening. Now her stomach lurched for a different reason. What *had* he done?

Ty edged closer and motioned Eddie to the trunk. Eddie looked sick but headed towards the car. "Wait, I've got an idea." He headed past them and she returned her glare to Ty.

"Talk. Now."

"Okay, look, it's not a big deal." He gestured to the trunk, but then turned his face away again, blanching at the stink coming from the backpack she'd dropped. The smell had lessened with their distance, but only barely. She resisted the urge to take a deep breath.

"Eddie and I bought some fireworks last night, on the Indian reservation, when we went to the casino. And we brought some stuff to, you know, make dogs not smell them, if we had to cross a border or something." He gestured vaguely towards Oregon.

"You...wait. Illegal fireworks. You bought *illegal* fireworks and put them *in my car.*" Hysteria might have tinged the last few words of that sentence as the implications of what he'd done hit her. Now was *not* the time to be transporting illegal fireworks across state lines. Okay, there was *no* time to be transporting illegal fireworks across state lines, but now was really, really not the time. She'd be under extra scrutiny until an offer was made, and then again until she'd proven herself in the new position. She wasn't exactly sure where fireworks fell in the code of ethics of certified financial planners, but she *was* sure that she didn't want to find out.

"You all need any help?" she heard, and snapped her head around.

It was him. Her sexy maybe-cop, maybe-insurance, maybe-whatever-the-hell guy. And he was heading her way. Her certainty that he'd been eyeing her purely as a woman fled, and now he really did look like a cop.

Shit, shit, shit. No, no, no. Go, go, go!

"No, Ivy—" Ty started, but she was *not* in the mood.

"You, no talking." She jabbed a finger into his chest. "We're fine, thank you!" she called to the approaching man, seeing the exact second that the noxious stench reached him. His already white face turned an interesting shade of pasty gray and he jerked to a stop. He'd barely stepped into the road, on the other side of the street, which meant the smell was even worse than she'd realized. He took another step, then seemed to think better of it.

"All good!" She tried to find a smile that was enough to reassure him, but not strong enough to encourage him to come closer.

Eddie ran up, ripping open a box of heavy-duty black trash bags. He was wearing bright yellow rubber kitchen gloves. She glanced over at the man to see his reaction. He'd cocked his head and was still watching, but made no move to come closer.

"Shit, Ivy, I can't believe you broke the whole bottle," Eddie was saying as he scooped the backpack into a trash bag and tied it closed. He leaned over like he was going to vomit, but managed to hold it back. Then he used another trash bag to enclose the first. And then another. "This was concentrated, we only used one tiny drop on the box, now you busted the whole bottle."

It was hard to look like she was about to breathe fire when taking such shallow breaths, but she was sure she'd accomplished it when Eddie turned to look up at her from his crouch on the ground and blanched at her expression. He went for a fourth trash bag.

Ty was holding a hand over his nose and looking down at the ground. "Uh, Ivy, do you have any other shoes with you?"

She looked down. There were was an oily spot the size of a dime on her sneaker. Fuck.

Glaring at him, she toed off the splattered shoe. "Grab my bag."

By the time he came back with her suitcase, she had both shoes off, as well as the sock from the foot that had caught the oil. That foot was resting on her clean sneaker. She pulled flip-flops out of the outside zippered pocket on her suitcase, and tossed the stained shoe at Eddie, not minding in the least when it hit him in his ribs.

Ty picked up her other shoe and the socks and brought them to Eddie, before she could throw those as well. She marched to the driver's seat and clenched the steering wheel for several moments. She would not drive upset. She could still smell the skunk scent, but it wasn't nearly as bad as it had been. Finally able to take a deep breath, she forced her body to relax. She had a six-hour drive ahead of her, she needed to be level-headed. She pulled out her phone and searched her playlists, while she ignored Eddie climbing in behind her and Ty dropping her suitcase next to him, then getting into the front passenger seat.

She found her angry playlist, set it to shuffle, and turned up the volume. Without a word, she headed towards Oregon.

An hour later, she turned the volume down to a level that was more normal when there were passengers in the car who might want to hear each other. The boys both visibly relaxed, though they waited before saying anything. She'd had time to think. Time to consider that fireworks were not illegal on the reservation, so buying them was not illegal. But that whole legal-on-a-reservation-but-not-in-the-state-the reservation-existed-in thing was confusing as hell. And certainly not something she'd ever taken the time to research.

Still, having them in her car was not illegal. She didn't think. She'd been so busy running she hadn't even thought to tell the guys to throw the damn things out. Driving them to another state...*probably not illegal?* She wasn't totally sure. She didn't think so, though, or she'd be pulling over and finding a dumpster now. Only setting them off, in Oregon, would be illegal. Probably. So, it was fine. Everything was fine.

"What the fuck were you thinking?" she finally said, the first words spoken since she'd started driving.

"They are *not* illegal," Ty began. "I swear, we got them at the regular fireworks stand. The *legal* stand, we weren't buying them in some back alley."

"Not illegal in Idaho, you mean. Definitely illegal in Oregon. Actually, they're probably not even legal in Idaho, off the reservation. And you obviously aren't planning on setting them off on the reservation, unless you have another trip planned for next week?"

She hadn't even considered the fact that the Fourth of July was next week when the boys had asked if they could come with her, to visit the casino. Obviously *they'd* thought about it, and made plans.

"Where did you get the smelly shit?"

"Online."

Of course.

"And you put it on the box in case we happened to get pulled over by canine police? Without telling me you were putting *me* and *my car* at risk?"

"We were thinking of the inspection crossing."

She blinked. "The inspection crossing. Between states? You thought there was a border crossing between Washington and Oregon?"

"Well, yeah," Eddie mumbled.

"You didn't notice that we didn't go through any on our way *into* Washington? Or Idaho?"

"Yeah, but we figured better safe than sorry. Since we had the stuff anyway."

"You thought it would be okay to make my car smell like skunk."

"I only used a drop," Ty reminded her. "And I was going to offer to wash your car when we got home. And we did move your suitcase out of the trunk."

He said it like he was expecting her to thank him, and sighed when she shot him a glare.

Border stations and illegal fireworks. *Idiots.* Actually, she had a vague memory of going through an interstate inspection station once, on a road trip with her parents and Ty, to the Grand Canyon. Maybe when they drove into California from Nevada? She'd been a teenager, but she kind of remembered something like that. She had a vague idea that it had something to do with fruit.

Sighing, she rolled her shoulders and tried to release the remaining tension. This was fine. She was pretty sure they hadn't done anything illegal. "You owe me a pair of sneakers."

"Fine."

"I can't believe you took advantage of my road trip like this. My *work* trip."

"It's not illegal," Ty repeated.

"Then why the skunk spray?"

"Just a precaution," Eddie assured her.

"Mm-hm. And what, you're going to throw the fireworks away when we get home? You just thought it would be nice to donate that money to our Native American neighbors?"

"Uh, no?" Eddie was back to mumbling.

"Those kinds of fireworks are illegal for a reason," she reminded them. "You want to start a fire? Be responsible for burning down trees, homes, maybe even killing some people?"

"We're going to set them off at the beach," Ty told her. "You know my buddy Jack is a firefighter. It's his party, he's got it all planned, perfectly safe. Everyone chipped in for the stuff."

"Yeah, right. You convince Mom and Dad about that, and I won't interfere."

"Ivy, no, you can't tell them. We're all adults here and it's none of their business."

"Ty."

He sighed and turned to look out the side window.

Okay, she wasn't going to tattle on her brother. But she was sure going to have a conversation with firefighter Jack. She just wouldn't be able to live with herself if she was even tangentially responsible for a fire.

The forest clearing was suddenly lit with a colorful display, as one of the teenagers set off a mini-fountain of a firework. The pack didn't do fireworks every year. The biggest factors were wind and dryness, but this year, the wind was calm and they'd enjoyed a late spring, so the fireworks were on, and the kids were delighted. The clearing had been prepared and several adults were in charge of keeping an eye on the fire hazard, but Brad wasn't one of them, so he got to sit back and watch the fun.

They'd enjoyed a lazy afternoon picnic at the pack house, where he, Molly and Taylor had handled the burgers and brats while an energetic game of flag football, complete with Chester and Samuel as coaches, competed to drown out the teenagers having fun with the stereo system and some kind of dance challenge.

He saw that Ryder, who'd been asleep in his father's lap not twenty minutes ago, had woken up and was staring wide-eyed at the fireworks, though he edged closer to his sister Alexis when one let off a piercing whistle. The little girl hugged him close, smiling in delight at the display, and something deep in Brad's heart eased.

He'd worried when she'd first joined the pack, after they'd rescued her from the fuckers who had kidnapped her. Worried because she hadn't acted like the little girl she was. Not that he was an expert, but even as she'd started to relax into their pack, talk more and interact, she always seemed older than her nine years. Not that he'd blamed her. Getting kidnapped by a sadistic fuck like Ken Cage would scar anyone, let alone a sweet girl who'd led a normal, innocent life until that point.

But rescuing her—and he was damn thankful he'd been in on that takedown and seen the punishments meted out—had only been the start. Watching her open up and join the Jenner family, join the pack life, had been a blessing. Seeing her now, just over a year later, in such a carefree and happy moment, had him damn near choking up.

Theo dropped into the camp chair next to him, pulling him away from memories of last year's action. Though they were in the security business, that kind of drama was rare for them to be involved in. Life had quieted down a lot since he'd left the Army, and he wasn't one bit sorry about that. His life was mostly running security checks for businesses that hired their firm, though he and the other guys could be called in for bodyguard duty when the occasion called for it.

He'd liked that Mountain View Pack owned their own security company, so he could use the skills he'd learned as an Army Ranger, be a contributing member of the pack. Having come from Boston, he was used to snow and cold weather, but he hadn't been prepared for the sheer beauty of the territory that encompassed parts of Washington, Idaho and Montana. He'd been here just over three years now, and had never regretted his choice to move here and join Mountain Pack.

"It was a good day," Theo said, handing Brad a beer.

He opened the beer and took an appreciative pull. "It was. I worked the last two Fourth of Julys. Nice to get to hang with the pack this year."

"It was hella hot last year, you timed it well my friend."

He laughed. "All intentional, I assure you."

It was full dark now, so he lifted his face to the light of the moon. It was waxing, only a crescent, but it was bright. He felt the faint tingle of magic that reminded him he was a werewolf. Not that he ever forgot. He'd been born a werewolf, part of a pack—but only just, as his parents preferred to live in the city. He'd gone to human schools, then joined the Army the day he'd graduated high school. He'd put in his years, but there was no way he could hide what he was for a full career. Figuring out a way to change into a wolf most months was hard enough. Hiding his extra strength, stamina, better healing, slower aging, that was too much of a challenge, so he'd gotten out at twenty-six.

It had taken the best part of a year to research packs and finally settle on this one. Going back to Boston wasn't in the running. Nor was he interested in re-joining the pack despite the fact that most of them lived in a rural area, which was what he was looking for.

His brother Ian was down in Los Angeles, but no way was Brad going back to *any* city. He wanted to act like a wolf. Feel like a wolf. Live like a wolf. Okay, not really, but like a person who could, and did, change into a wolf, and wanted to run through the forests. His whole life he'd had to pretend to be something other than what he was. And sure, even here, he couldn't exactly waltz into the nearby towns as a wolf, or show up at his clients' businesses and howl at the moon. But there was plenty of time he could spend here, with the pack, being himself, and that was what he'd craved.

"So, you still refraining from being a creeper?" Theo asked.

Brad growled at him.

Hillary, carrying another camp chair, stopped next to them. "Why is Brad growling?"

Theo grinned and motioned for their alpha to take a seat. "You'll like this. He met a girl."

"Ooh, tell me everything." She opened her chair, plopped down, and leaned towards Brad.

"I did not meet a girl," he protested, smacking Theo's shoulder while debating on if he was actually annoyed or not.

As his pack alpha, Hillary could force him to tell her everything. But she wouldn't. Not unless something very serious was going on. She respected her wolves, respected their privacy, but also cared about them and wanted what was best for them. And, as someone who'd mated just over a year ago, to their other alpha, Zach, Larry believed that mating would make all of her wolves happier. Not a theory that Brad subscribed to, but he'd never tell that to Hillary.

"He saw a girl, and considered stalking her, but talked himself out of it," Theo responded.

Brad dropped his head into his hands. It was either that or punch his friend, and that wouldn't go over well at a family party.

Hillary laughed, patting his knee, able to tell through their pack bonds that he was more exasperated than angry. "Now I really want to hear all about it. Her."

"So last week, Mr. Smooth here was—"

"Dude. You weren't even there."

"Fine, you tell it."

Sighing, Brad took a long pull from his beer and leaned back in his chair. "Last week when I was doing that security evaluation for the title company that was vandalized here in town, I saw a woman." He shot a glare at Theo. "A *woman*, not a girl, and she caught my interest." He ran a hand over the back of his neck, shot a glance at Hillary, who was watching him expectantly. He wasn't exactly sure how to explain what he'd felt. "I guess she twigged something in me. My *instincts*," he emphasized as Theo snorted. "Could be something about the security check. Maybe something seemed off and subconsciously I considered her a suspect. She was definitely worried about being caught, whatever she was doing."

"Hm." Hillary pursed her lips. "Seems to me like you have a pretty good handle on your security instincts, and you'd be able to identify if that was what was pinging you. Was she pretty?"

He slanted her a look. She wasn't wrong. He hadn't been thinking security issues.

"Gorgeous." Theo looked smug.

"You saw her?" Hillary asked.

"No, but I can read my boy. Tell me I'm wrong."

She was. Glowing brown skin, dark hair that fell past her shoulders, wide eyes that had seemed to see right into him. The clinical part of his brain had pegged her at five foot nine, one hundred seventy pounds. The male part of his brain had taken in the whole package and been very impressed. And very interested.

"Anyway," Brad said. "I was hoping to get closer to her when my walk-through was over, see if I could get a better sense of why she was on my radar. But Bernard needed some reassurances, and by the time I made it back outside, she'd left the cafe. I heard shouting, and the two guys she'd been eating with were running to her. There was some kind of altercation at the trunk of her car."

He finished his beer, set the can under his chair. "I started to head over there, and the look on her face...I know guilty and panicked when I see it, okay? There is no question that's what she was. The guys were also acting sketchy. Nervous. I only made it a couple of steps, and..." He blinked at the memory of the overwhelming stench that had kept him from getting closer. He'd thought about that day several times now, wondered if he should have just kept going, despite the smell, but he was pretty sure he would have vomited, and what good could that have done?

He knew his sense of smell was better than a normal human's, but he wasn't sure how the three of them had managed to stand there amidst the extremely foul stench that had permeated the whole street.

"They must have had some of that skunk musk you can buy in a bottle. Or else they had an entire family of skunks in that trunk. One or the other. Add that to the guilty looks, the nervous mannerisms? Those three were hiding something, for sure. From me, specifically? I don't think so. I think me being there was a coincidence. And I don't think it had anything to do with the vandalism at the title company. Which is *why*," he gave Theo a hard look, though the other man seemed entirely unconcerned, "I have not tracked her down."

"Because you think if you do, you'll be a creeper," Theo said. "Showing up at her door, all 'hey, didn't I see you at that cafe three hundred miles from here? Have time for a chat?'"

Basically. "She'd think I was investigating her. And she wouldn't be wrong, would she?"

"Could you find her?" Hillary asked.

Theo snorted again. "Of course he could."

He met Hillary's gaze. "Yeah. I got her license number. Oregon plates, which is why Theo knows she'd be several hundred miles away."

"So, let me just make sure we're all thinking the same thing here. You were drawn to her before she did anything suspicious. So, we're wondering if it was just because she was attractive, because she was exhibiting suspicious behavior, but so subtly that only your instincts picked up on it, or...she's your mate."

It was his turn to snort. "There's no reason to think that last part."

"No? Is there any reason to think it's *not* that last part?"

"Sure. Going purely by the percentages, the chances are negligible. First, just the chances I would randomly spot my mate sitting at a cafe in some Podunk town in Idaho, and not know it. Because I definitely wasn't standing there thinking, *oh, wow, there's my mate.* But more, she was human. I'm one hundred percent certain of it. And you know the chances of a mate being human are much smaller than finding your mate at all."

"Not 'some Podunk town in Idaho'. *Your* Podunk town in Idaho." Theo looked like he'd just delivered a game-winning answer, as if that somehow made everything obvious.

A warm hand settled on Brad's shoulder, and he felt a tension he hadn't realized had been growing in him, seep away. Zach, Hillary's mate, his alpha.

Hillary was studying him, and he could guess at the reason. Why was he getting worked up? Why was this something he was still thinking about, more than a week later? Why was he having to tell himself, multiple times a day, that he couldn't go stalk this woman, that it would be inappropriate as hell? How had she gotten under his skin, when they'd never spoken beyond shouts across a street, barely made eye contact? *Fuuuuck.*

While he was ruminating on all of that, Hillary was giving Zach a quick summary of the situation. Brad scrubbed his suddenly tired eyes with the heels of his hands.

"Look, Brad," she said, bringing him back into the conversation. "I agree with you that a random human spotting a pretty woman on the street and using her license plate to track her down would be creepy. Absolutely. But, the thing is, you're not human. And while you can, and should, play by the human rules most of the time, I think mates are an exception to that. Because mating *is magic.* There's no denying that. If what you were sensing was a mate bond, then it's in both of your best interests to find her. You're a great guy. I would be devastated to learn that a lovely woman had a chance to be your mate, and lost out on the magic of that because of, well, skunks."

Brad thought about what Hillary had said as he lay in bed, trying to get to sleep. He had work in the morning. Plus, he honestly felt like an idiot, laying here thinking about a girl. *Woman*. Mooning like some lame-ass teenager ruled by his hormones.

But see...that was the thing that wouldn't let him get to sleep. First was the fact that he *did* have a good handle on his instincts when it came to danger. He'd been a fucking Ranger, for fuck's sake, and been damn good at it. He'd been in security ever since. He *trusted* his instincts. Knew those danger-related instincts. And those had not been the instincts firing that day in town. Sure, at the end, when the boys had started yelling and the woman was darting frantic looks as he started to head over. But before that...no. Definitely not danger vibes.

And second was the fact that what had kept him looking over at her, had made him want to have a chat with her, was his gut. Not his cock. Not the churning of his gut that told him something was off, something was wrong. It had been a new feeling, one he'd never experienced before.

Put those two facts together, and, well, he wasn't sure Hillary was wrong. She was pretty smart, and she'd been through the mating process. The idea had been at the back of his mind for days, but he'd refused to give it focus. Now, though, he couldn't shove the thought away again.

What it really came down to was, *if* the woman was his mate, did he *want* to find her? Most wolves he knew would never ask that question. They searched their whole lives for their mates. That special someone with whom they could forge a solid bond. Not just an emotional bond, like most lovers or partners. But an actual metaphysical bond, allowing the mates to feel each other, deep in their souls.

As Hillary had said, it was magic. He couldn't claim to understand it, but then again, he didn't really understand how he turned into a wolf every month. It made no fucking sense, honestly. And yet it happened. As did mates. Most wolves revered that connection, at least as far as he could tell. He'd not had deep conversations about it with his buddies or anything. But in his experience, that soul-deep bond wasn't always a good thing.

Shit. He sat up and swung his legs over the side of the bed, braced his arms on his thighs. He was aware that his upbringing wasn't particularly normal for werewolves. It wasn't unheard of, but not usual. His parents had raised him and his brothers mostly outside of the pack. Sure, they'd had to trek into the forest a few times a year for pack events. The alphas had insisted, much to his mother's annoyance. She preferred city living, surrounded by humans who had no idea what she was. What they all were—his parents, he and his two brothers. She hadn't cared that he'd had to give up playing sports, because it was too hard to constantly regulate his speed and strength to that of the other kids. He'd managed it through middle school, but those puberty hormones had been a bitch.

She hadn't cared that they'd only had each other to run with most full moons, as she and his father had gone off to do their own thing, leaving him to take care of Ian and Declan. In Paige Burke's world, everyone existed to enhance and improve her life. And her mate, bonded soul to soul, wanted only to ensure that what she wanted was what she got.

Her sons hadn't been mistreated. Hadn't been abused. They'd just...existed only to give her happiness, something they all too often failed at.

But. *But.* He was a fucking adult now, and he knew for damn sure his parents' relationship was not the norm. He suspected his mother was a narcissist. And that was not the fault of being a were-wolf, or of the mate bond. But the fact that his father was unable to deny his wife anything *was* due to the mate bond. Maybe.

Shit. Surging to his feet, he stripped off his boxers and concentrated hard, remembering the bright moon from earlier in the evening. He focused on that, pulled the memory of that light deep within himself, and shifted. It was slower than normal, since it wasn't the full moon and he wasn't with pack. But it got the job done. He shook himself, resettling the fur on his now four-legged body. He used the doggy door in the living room and loped out of the house, off the deck, and into the surrounding forest. In this form, his instincts were closer to the surface. And things were simpler.

Maybe the woman wasn't his mate. But there was only one way to know.

Hiding from it would solve the problem, but not in a way that he was comfortable with. He needed to find her, needed to know. Then he could determine if she was someone he could be with. Someone he could risk his soul for. It was time to find out.

Find purchase links for Wolf Called at https://www.kbalan.com/books/wolf-called

To join KB Alan's newsletter, visit www.kbalan.com/newsletter
Subscribers will receive a link to download a free copy of Past Perfect, a prequel to the Perfect Fit series

ALSO BY KB ALAN

Perfect Fit Series (Erotic Romance)

Perfect Formation (Book 1)

Perfect Alignment (Book 2)

Perfect Stranger (Book 2.5)

Perfect Addition (Book 3)

Perfect Temptation (Book 4)

Fully Invested (Contemporary Romance)

(Part of the Wildlife Ridge World)

Coming Home (Book 1)

Breaking Free (Book 2)

Finding Forever (Book 3)

Wolf Appeal Series (Paranormal Romance)

Alpha Turned (Book 1)

Challenge Accepted (Book 2)

Going Deeper (Book 3)

Wolf Called (Book 4)

Stand Alone

Bound by Sunlight (Erotic Romance)

Keeping Claire (Fantasy Romance)

Sweetest Seduction (Contemporary Romance)

www.kbalan.com

ABOUT THE AUTHOR

KB Alan lives the single life in Southern California. She acknowledges that she should probably turn off the computer and leave the house once in a while in order to find her own happily ever after, but for now she's content to delude herself with the theory that Mr. Right is bound to come knocking at her door through no real effort of her own. Please refrain from pointing out the many flaws in this system. Other comments, however, are happily received.

www.kbalan.com

To join KB's newsletter, visit www.kbalan.com/newsletter
Subscribers will receive a link to download a free copy of Past Perfect, a prequel to the Perfect Fit series

f facebook.com/kbalan
🐦 twitter.com/KB_Alan
📷 instagram.com/authorkbalan
BB bookbub.com/authors/kb-alan

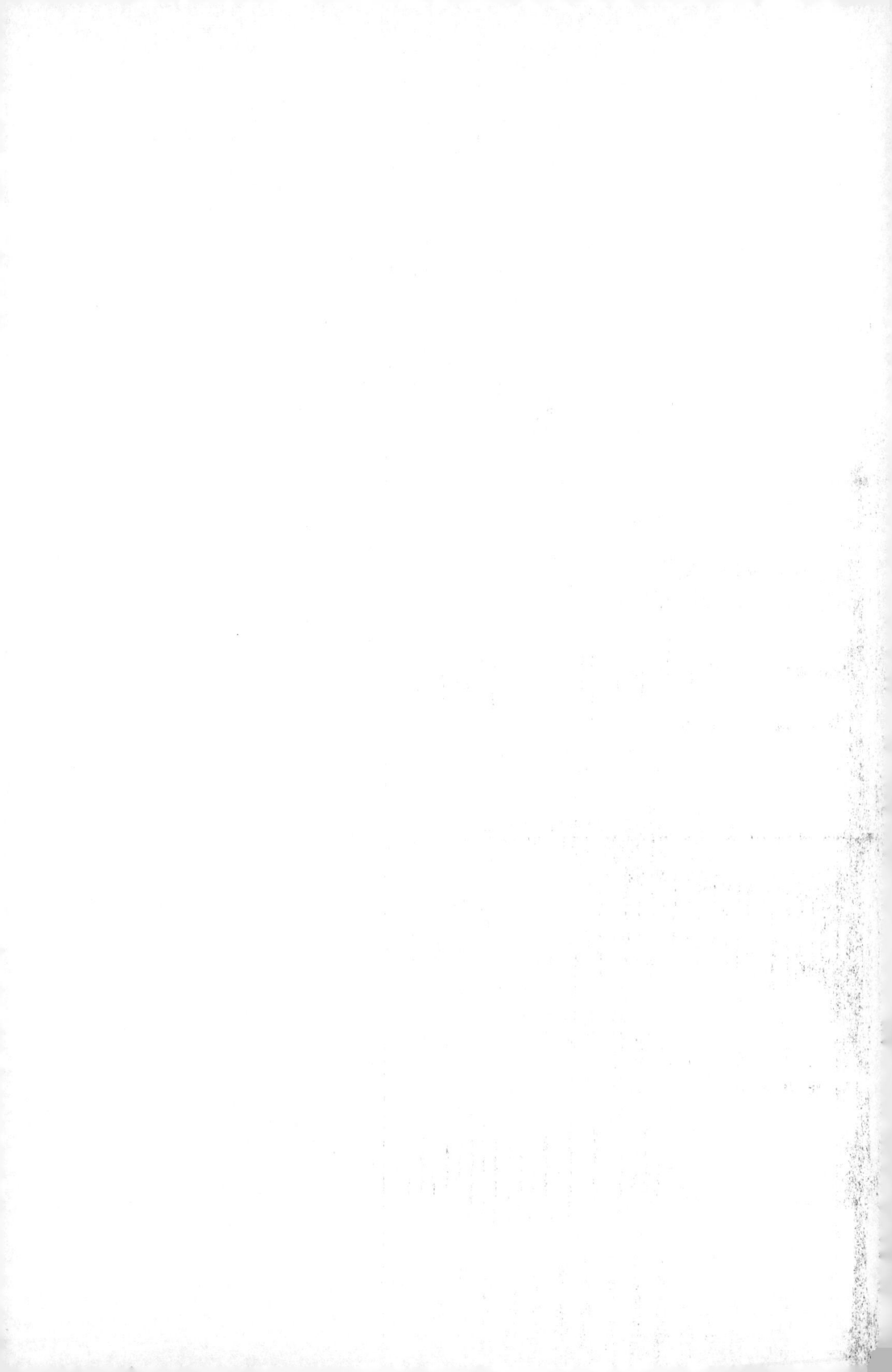

Printed in Great Britain
by Amazon